SPREAD SOME LOVE

RELATIONSHIPS 101

REVISED EDITION

JOHN A. ANDREWS

NATIONAL BESTSELLING AUTHOR

BOOKS THAT WILL ENHANCE YOUR LIFE

Published in the U.S.A. by
Books That Will Enhance Your Life™
www.BooksThatWillEnhanceYourLife.com

ISBN: 978-0-98384576-8

Cover Design: John A. Andrews
Cover Photo: Adrian Carr
Edited by: A L I

SPREAD SOME LOVE

RELATIONSHIPS 101

This book is dedicated to the woman:
Who, first taught me about relationships;
Instilled true values in me;
Encouraged, guided and lifted me;
The one who gave me life,
A leader and lover of many…
My mother, a true legend,
Elaine Louisa Andrews
&
To the lady in my life - Jannise,
Thanks for bringing out the best in me.

Contents

If
a person isn't willing to work on him or herself they should stay out of the falling in love business; the world is full of too many abandoned relationships and broken hearts.

- *John A. Andrews*

Introduction

Alan Loy McGuinnis states in his book *The Friendship Factor* "The best relationships are built up, like a fine lacquer finish, with the accumulated layers of many acts of kindness."[1] A love weaved with many strands tend to be stronger than the one done with a few strands. Love in action moves people versus a love that is sitting on the fence.

People go to extremes just to find love. If you were to watch a house plant as it grows you'll notice that it will always tend to grow towards the sunlight. If you manually changed its course - as time goes by it would gradually move back towards the sunlight. So is it with love. Love seeks illumination; it wants to be kept alive, it wants to flourish.

A young couple, madly in love but lacking the "green thumb" effect, told me about a situation with one of their house plants. The plant was put outside after being housebound for several years. They claimed that in less than a few days an enormous flower bloomed from the once seemed barren plant.

The plant produced when exposed to the light.

Love is life. It gives life to darkness, transforming while it enhances.

The new you will emerge like the stream or conduit of ever-flowing love when you decide to change. Firstly deciding to love yourself: by finding value in yourself, and secondly giving love away - placing value in others. This is classified as a double win; you win by helping others win.

Some of the principles shared herein may sound as if they are an "Old School" philosophy. The "New School" could say: "this doesn't apply in today's society." Well, the fact remains that if years ago you were to literally jump off the top of a tall building - that would have been very, very, very tragic. So, why would you even consider entertaining the thought that if you were to try that feat today that a net would spring out of nowhere and catch you?

My desire for this volume is that you would treat it as a smorgasbord – use what you need. Methods change but principles last – they are forever. More than 60% of my relations are from the "New Fraternity" and I've noticed how "those acquaintances" struggle keeping their relationships intact without the implementation of these values.

This is not just another book on friendship, love, marriage and sex. Neither do the philosophies presented herein represent new methods, but principles - dominant since the beginning of time. They contain ethics missing in every failed marriage and every unhealthy relationship where applicable. Even if the principles may upset some of today's popular habits, there is one advantage: They work! As a divorcee, dad, entrepreneur and life coach, it's not just that I believe so but I know they do.

Several ingredients go into the baking of a cake. This book, written for the millions of people who would like to master love, find the lover they desire or grow together with the one they have, contains principles to keep love alive. Take away one principle and love sits on the fence. Could you imagine if you were to omit an important ingredient such as the baking soda from the cake's recipe? What kind of cake would you have?

If you are married, planning on doing so or desire to coach on marriage, all of these philosophies should go into the recipe. On the other hand, if you want to just live a life of love that is always flowing and growing, the icing and the sprinkles may be too sweet for you, but you can still enjoy the rest of this volume.

If you are a man looking for true love, your preparation is paramount. You want to be ready when that opportunity presents itself. And if you are a woman looking for that Mr. Right, no longer will you claim "a good man is hard to find" you will recognize if he is a catch or a throwback.

-- John A. Andrews

"Love
is, without question, life's
greatest experience"[1]

-Napoleon Hill

1

THE LOVE FACTOR

What really is Love? What's this all powerful emotion which makes one give up his crown for the one he loves? In his book *Think and Grow Rich* Napoleon Hill introduces us to Mrs. Wallis Simpson who caused the king to relinquish his crown for her love. Wallis possessed a burning desire to find a mate and searched carefully every step of the way. Her primary pursuit was love. She knew exactly what she wanted, not after she met the Prince of Wales, but long before. Despite her failure to find it twice she had courage enough to continue. Though shadowed by her obscurity, Wallis triumphed over long odds until she finally met the king.[2]

Love will cause one to go to other limits as in the case of Alfredo and Juliet, according to Shakespeare. **Love** is by far the most powerful force on earth. "For love, we will climb mountains, cross seas, traverse desert sands, and endure hardships. Without love, mount-ains become unclimbable, seas uncrossable, deserts unbearable, and hardships our plight in life."[3] States Dr. Gary Chapman in his book *The Five Love Languages*.

The best definition to this all powerful force is summed up in the bible (1 Cor.13:4-8 KJV), "Though I speak with the tongues of men and of angels, and have not charity, I am become as sounding brass, or a tinkling cymbal. And though I have the gift of prophecy, and understand all mysteries, and all knowledge; and though I have all faith, so that I could remove mountains, and have not charity, I am nothing. And though I bestow all my goods to feed the poor, and though I give my body to be burned, and have not charity, it profiteth me nothing. Charity suffereth long, and is kind; charity envieth not; charity vaunteth not itself, is not puffed up, Doth not behave itself unseemly, seeketh not her own, is not easily provoked, thinketh no evil; Rejoiceth not in iniquity, but rejoiceth in the truth; Beareth all things, believeth all things, hopeth all things, endureth all things. Charity never faileth: but whether there be prophecies, they shall fail; whether there be tongues, they shall cease; whether there be knowledge, it shall vanish away."

The famous Vince Lombardi, late coach of the Green Bay Packers echoed: "Winning is not a sometime thing; it's an all time thing. You don't win once in a while, you don't do things right once in a while, you do them right all the time. Winning is habit. Unfortunately, so is losing."[4] As a player Lombardi demanded the best from himself. With such a relational quality, no wonder he was one of the best coaches in the game of football, gaining respect not only from his peers but by players alike.

Loving is synonymous with winning, hating is not. Caring is not a once in a while thing but a forever endeavor. To love and be loved demands your best. In these pages you will find yourself, the "new self" you never knew existed. When you do, like to an oasis in a desert you will lead others to drink and they too will return and bring others; quenching the thirst of multitudes of love thirsty individuals.

When love like a fire is ablaze in one's heart and soul, it spreads, engulfing the possessor and recipient in flames of brilliance.

So many false pretenders or people possessing hypocritical love treat love like a light switch, they turn this valuable asset on and off only to find themselves falling short, realizing that love is not flowing. If it is not flowing it is dying, and like the stream without its source, one cannot give something which he does not first possess.

We all know that a stream is unable to deliver to the ocean if its supply is aborted by a deficiency such as a drought or a dam. Cure the drought of love and it flows, release the dam and it gushes out. I like looking at a cloudless sky but also like to see the clouds so full that they cannot contain anymore rain. Those clouds cannot provide rain if they are empty and the more laden they are the more showers they deposit. As my mom used to say "some-thing can't come from nothing."
What the world needs today is a divine love - one so high and so deep that would withstand the tests of time. This love starts with you, right where you are; for in order to love someone else it's imperative that you first love yourself.

Love styles

In today's society love is usually viewed from several different approaches or Love Styles.

"Love styles are models of lovers developed by John Lee (1973, 1988). He identified six basic theories - also known as "colors" of love - that people use in their interpersonal relationships:

- Eros – a passionate physical and emotional love based on aesthetic enjoyment; stereotype of romantic love.
- Ludus – a love that is played as a game or sport; conquest
- Storge – an affectionate love that slowly develops from friendship, based on similarity
- Pragma – love that is driven by head, not the heart, undemonstrative
- Mania – highly volatile love; obsession; Fueled by low self esteem
- Agape – selfless altruistic love; spiritual; Motherly love

Clyde Hendrick and Susan Hendrick of Texas Tech University have conducted extensive research on the love styles since the mid-1980s. They have found that men tend to be more ludic, whereas women tend to be storgic and pragmatic. Mania is often the first love style teenagers display. Relationships based on similar love styles were found to last longer. People often look for people with the same love style as themselves for a relationship."[5]

Regardless of your love styles, what you love and how you love defines you.

Love by example

All too familiar is this statement: "In order to be a friend; you must first become friendly." Jesus commands: "A new commandment I give you, that ye love one another; as I have loved you, that ye also love one another. By this all men shall know that you are my disciples, if ye have love one to another." (John 13:34-35 KJV) The people who create long lasting meaningful friendships with others understand that love lives on long after they're gone and therefore they're not afraid to invest in meaningful associations. They understand that now is all the time they have. There is no time for hatred or false pretense. So they give 150% to their relationships.

False pretense

Mr. Z, grew up with a gold spoon in his mouth. His parent's inheritance was an ever flowing source. He had been married for several years to the woman he referred to as his trophy wife. She's a smart and talented woman, who loves her 4 kids all under the age of 10. His kids attend the best schools, and yet, they are rude and ill-mannered. His offspring adopt the "monkey see monkey do" philosophy, and bear fruits after his kind, he, knowing or unknowingly is harvesting a generation of future "play-haters" or "hypo-critical lovers."

I first met the family over 5 years ago when I was brought on to be their chauffeur. They had just about everything that money can buy and travels frequently enjoying their "lifestyle." Yet they were miserable. Their marriage had gradually turned into a disaster.

I noticed that on some of those trips with Mr. Z, that he was having affairs. He knew that I despised it, but I felt trapped. It was not long before love in his home started to wane. Depression stepped in intensified by his wife's bitterness. They yelled and screamed at each other frequently. Their kids felt dishonored and escalated their rebellion. Disrespect in the home grew to an all time high. Not wanting to continue as an abettor I recently gave up that job to someone else.

Their relationship has eventually cascaded into a huge breakup for the courts to decide how their kids are to be raised, among other things. It is unfortunate but so many kids are thrown into these unwarranted parental conflicts.

First love

This book will be incomplete if it didn't feature the character Mr. X, whose mom played a major role in his life by teaching him love in action.

As a kid, he had the opportunity of seeing this special quality exhibited seven out of seven. Although the words "I love you" were seldom heard from his parents lips, his mom always let her action do the talking. Despite being a victim of poor education, and being responsible for a house filled with nine kids, she became known as a legend in her community because she not only cared but cared deeply.

She wasted not a single moment working endlessly and tirelessly by day, and nightly encouraging all nine around a kerosene lamp (back then they didn't have electricity). She wanted all her kids to be endowed, in their chosen calling with opportunities which she never had. With smoke in their eyes they burned the midnight oil in their effort to excel. When their dad passed on in 1967, a financial reverse began, she fought through it and with some of her meager resources saw Mr. X through most of high school.

Despite not having riches, but only just enough, along with a busy lifestyle, she found time to open her door to a stranger, neighbor or friend - providing them with a warm meal while she articulated about God's unfailing love. She cared for the sick, and the needy, shared groceries with them and most of all communicated her faith in God. Mr. X witnessed many lives changed; because his mom gave unselfishly. Although they didn't have all the gadgets as other kids did back then, she taught them how to share whatever little they had.

Her multiple battles with Alzheimer's disease for almost two decades ended in 2005. How-ever, her undying love lives on today and will for many generations due to her enormous love deposits into the lives of others.

Although Mr. X grew up poverty stricken and went to school at times without shoes on his feet, he studied and worked hard. During his adult years he read just about every personal development book he could get his hands on. While others were taking time off, he hustled and thus outworked everyone he encountered, taking their excuses away. Driven to succeed in whatever he does Mr. X sees value in the beggar, the downtrodden as well as the President. He knows how to befriend them. No wonder his winning ways create for him a successful environment anywhere he goes. Not only do people look to him to remold their lives and character but they know that they can count on him during crunch time.

A friend in need

Genuine friendship is at the root of all long lasting relationships. Have you ever noticed that whenever you are in need that real friends step up to the plate without being summoned? In my book *The 5 Steps To Changing Your Life*, I introduced the readers to my friend who is a movie producer, let's call him Mr. Y. He and I connected through our sons, and our friend-ship is speedily entering a full decade; he is like a friend and a brother. I have seen him get back on the horse and ride with passion and purpose after his divorce - to a life of respect and affluence.

Mr. Y and I do not talk everyday yet whenever he has an event, whether celebratory or other-wise I am always in attendance. It just seems to work out that way and through the years of our deep rooted friendship, his generosity to me has been a flowing stream.

Mr. Y. almost missed his flight

One day I was driving Mr. Y to LAX airport, he was flying out to a business meeting on the East Coast. As our limo pulled up close to the departure terminal I glanced into the rearview mirror and saw flashing lights from a trailing police cruiser. I pulled over to the curb. The investigating officer, after probing, searched the vehicle and subsequently called in airport authorities as backup. Mr. Y stood waiting in close proximity. I glanced in his direction and said "I'll be okay go ahead and catch your flight." He responded "I'm okay" waiting; he wanted to make sure that everything was handled satisfactorily.

The airport authorities arrived and could not find anything to cite me for. Therefore I was granted permission to leave. Mr. Y said his goodbyes and headed inside the terminal. His multi-millionaire status did not matter; he had been prepared to miss his flight if he had to, for his friend - me.

On another occasion Mr. Y. overheard me talking about my sons, now living on the East Coast, claiming how much they have missed me. He immediately stepped in, stating "John, you need to go and see your kids buddy" Knowing that they lived about 2,500 miles from Los Angeles, he offered to pick up the tab. I tried talking him out of it but he insisted that I find out the cost of the trip and pick up a check at his office the following day. I still had some reservation. The next day he called to find out what time I was dropping by. He wrote a check for my airfare, hotel accommodation and a rental car. That following week I spent seven days as a "full time dad" with my three sons. A week permanently etched in the recesses of my memory.

On the Saturday of my trip, it rained non stop. I mean, rain pelting down rain, the rain drops united with the glass window pane for a drum playing musical interlude. Nevertheless we braved the element, adventurously jumped inside the car and almost sailed to the pizzeria, grabbed two pies, returned to the hotel and watched four hours of all the new Disney episodics. During the pop corn break I discovered that the two eldest boys were writing a Disney–type screenplay. I became excitingly teary-eyed and during that emotion-al deluge I enthusiastically installed a writing software program on their laptop before going to bed that night.

The following morning I was awakened by bright lights accompanied by my boys enthusiastic chattering. I glanced in their direction; they were comedic as ever - filled with laughter. I was able to mask my laughter and asked "Why are you guys up so early?" They echoed "writing, writing our screenplay, what else daddy?" they were trying out the newly installed software program. That event brought tears to my eyes in what was a golden week in my life. Thanks to my friend Mr. Y. To him I'll be forever grateful.

Friendship in action

I have experienced similar situations with some of my other friends as well. When I resided in New York City back in the 80s, I bonded with a business associate, T.W. Those were the years before the beginning of my acting career, when I struggled with odd jobs and earned very little money - less than enough to get by. Through those tough times T.W. knew that if he ever needed a favor he could call on me; he knew I'd deliver and that standing in the gap for me was automatic.

During the summer of 2006, I was sitting in my Los Angeles apartment during the gas hike, my phone rang and it was T.W., we hadn't spoken in almost six months. He told me that he had run into some extra cash and wanted to send something my way. I tried not to admit my need of it, but it made him happy so I accepted his offer. My stops at the gas pump resulted in fill ups rather than a quarter of a tank for the next several months.

Intuition in friendship

My Jamaican friend W.B. is an amateur boxer and a physical fitness trainer. Our relationship goes back almost a decade. We first met while acting in a music video in Hollywood. I've noticed that he responds intuitively with a phone call to find out how I'm doing anytime someone jerks my chain. His intuition plays a major role in our friendship.

Henrik, a Swedish writer/producer not only gave me the starring role in one of his short films when he studied at AFI during my early days in Hollywood, but opened his doors to me when I became homeless after my divorce in 2000. Despite my many strike outs, he trusts my mentorship and his unfailing friendship lasts through the years.

My point is do good friends show up when you desperately need help? You bet! God, showed up in the fiery furnace with the three Hebrew boys, in the lions' den with Daniel, with the children of Israel crossing the red sea and today, he still shows up for you and me. His amazing, abundant, unconditional love is inexhaustible.

The golden rule in friendships

The golden rule in any relationship is: "Do unto others as you would have them do unto you." (Luke 6:31 NIV) "If ye fulfil the royal law according to the scripture, Thou shalt love the neighbor as thyself, ye do well." (James 2:8 KJV) But first let's deal with loving you; for it's impossible to have love for someone else if you do not…for yourself.

Know yourself

There is truth in this maxim: "To know me is to love me." -Unknown. Who are you, based on the experiences you've had in your past? Who are you when no one is watching? Who are you going to be in the future? If you find yourself in the deficit, ask yourself the question: "Am I willing to work on myself more than I do on the task with which I'm entrusted?"

Students study in order to maintain good grades. Pastors keep studying if they want to remain on the pulpit. Doctors and lawyers are known to study for almost a decade and beyond. No one wants an uneducated doctor to execute their heart transplant or an unskilled attorney to represent them in court. Yet, so many resist relational education and jump into "loving" relationships including marriage and expect the process of osmosis to build that relationship for them. They fail to continually equip themselves, not realizing that the largest room in our world today is the room for improvement and all that they can become beckons at them. Abraham Lincoln said: "Give me six hours to chop down a tree and I will spend the first four sharpening the axe."[6]

Once you know yourself it becomes a lot easier to see YOU in someone else, and creating that bond becomes a lot easier.

Love begins, or should begin at home. However, in most cases it does not; based on what is taught in that environment. In a normal situation love flows from the heart like a bonfire, setting another's heart on fire and when that blaze is concentrated it becomes difficult to contain love's flame.

Throughout my life I have encountered some great friends along with many "wannabe friends", the latter, because of their false pretense, weeded themselves out of my life when the going got tough. They lost that love which should have survived the tests of time. Give me five all weather friends and I'll create an army behind them – this is a vision which I cherish in every fiber of my being. A person's five closest friends say a lot about them and where they are heading whether uphill or downhill.

If you grasp this fact that loving starts with you, the way you love will have merit. It will be a higher and by all means - a deeper love. Even if you have come from a broken home, an abused relationship, poverty, communism, or atheism you can start right now with a clean slate and bring an abundance of love into your life and the lives of others.

Sacrificial love

What price are you willing to pay for those you love? So much that you will want to stand in the gap to protect those you genuinely care for. Permit me to rephrase. When it truly comes down to it, what price are you willing to pay for those you truly love? Is your love a sacrificial one?

A woman weighing only 95 pounds will attempt to lift up an eighteen wheeler if her little child was stuck under it.

Martin Luther King Jr. said "If a man hasn't discovered something he'll die for, he isn't fit to live."[7]

"Born in Atlanta, Georgia, Dr. Martin Luther King, Jr., graduated from Morehouse College (B.A., 1948), Crozer Theological Seminary (B.D., 1951), and Boston University (Ph.D., 1955). The son of the pastor of the Ebenezer Baptist Church in Atlanta, King was ordained in 1947 and became (1954) minister of a Baptist church in Montgomery, Alabama. He led the black boycott (1955-56) of segregated city bus lines and in 1956 gained a major victory and prestige as a civil-rights leader when Montgomery buses began to operate on a desegregated basis. King organized the Southern Christian Leadership Conference (SCLC), which gave him a base to pursue further civil-rights activities, first in the South and later nationwide.

His philosophy of nonviolent resistance led to his arrest on numerous occasions in the 1950s and 60s. His campaigns had mixed success, but the protest he led in Birmingham, Alabama, in 1963 brought him worldwide attention. He spearheaded the August 1963, *March on Washington,* which brought together more than 200,000 people. In 1964 he was awarded the Nobel Peace Prize. King's leadership in the civil-rights movement was challenged in the mid-1960s as others grew more militant. His interests, however, widened from civil rights to include criticism of the Vietnam War and a deeper concern over poverty. His plans for a Poor People's March to Washington were interrupted (1968) for a trip to Memphis, Tennessee, in support of striking sanitation workers.

On April 4, 1968, he was shot and killed as he stood on the balcony of the Lorraine Motel (since 1991 a civil-rights museum).[8]

Because of Dr. King's sacrificial love for his "cause" today black kids and white kids not only hold hands together, but Blacks and Whites are able to unite on several different agendas.

Love transforms

Some ask for more love but never release that which they have. It's like the stream drawing from the source but surrenders only to the dam.

John 3:16 (KJV) states, "For God so loved the world, that he gave his only begotten Son, that whosoever believeth in him should not perish, but have everlasting life."

God is love. He's the source which keeps giving to the stream continually. The people who think and do evil are like dead streams which misuse the source and therefore their freedom to love.

Love supports ones hopes and dreams and is never too tired to pass a compliment or do a good deed.

Love is like the sun which melts the iceberg of sin and mediocrity, molding and supporting our world.

Love is patient, strong and lasts forever.

Love is going the second mile. It does not judge; it forgives, building bridges between nations and failed relationships.

Love heals. It makes the flowers grow, and colors our world.

Love is passion, its desire, its creativity, its being and its doing. Love prospers, it elevates, it renovates and it electrifies.

Love builds up, it doesn't tear down.

Love brings light to darkness; it reaches through, sees through and follows through.

Love draws you closer to God. The higher and deeper your love, the higher and deeper is your relationship with God.

Love is patient however; it does not sit on the fence.

Love is never fragmented; it's an inseparable whole which does not delight in bits and pieces.

Love works because God is LOVE and always will be.

Your worst enemy

By not loving yourself you're destined to be your own worst enemy and thereby fail to discover what a wonderful person you are or could become.

Loving YOU starts with your self-confidence: that deep down feeling inside of you that lets you know that you have value. It is not an arrogant feeling but rather a combination of self-appreciation, self-respect and self-worth. When those qualities are discovered, you become self-forgiving and the new you emerge like a flower in springtime.

Loving yourself will take some self-discovery, self-development, self-discipline and some self-dedication. Are you willing to put in the work in order to reap the results?

In his book *Self-Love* author and preacher Robert H. Schuller lists Ten Steps to a Strong Self-Love:

- *Get rid of your fear of failure.*
- *Discover that unique person called you.*
- *Compliment yourself.*
- *Forgive yourself.*
- *Improve yourself.*
- *Accept yourself.*
- *Commit yourself to a great cause.*
- *Believe in success.*
- *Strive for excellence.*
- *Build self-love in others.*[9]

Once you have diagnosed the symptom and treated the disease you're on your way to total recovery - a winning character.

Create a winning character

How do you earn this all important stripe on your lapel? "You can get everything in life you want if you just help enough other people get what they want."[10] – Zig Ziglar.

In order to help someone get what they want you have to first listen to their needs. And that takes listening not only with the ear but with the heart. This is a skill which requires patience, understanding and wisdom. In some marriages wives complain a lot saying "my husband never listens to me." Whenever this happens it's a clear indication that the two hearts are not in sync and therefore her words enter his ears but not his mind, heart and soul. The fire in their hearts for each other has been extinguished through the years. Most of the time what she is saying is: "pay me some attention even if what I'm saying doesn't make any sense." Women, unlike most men tend to say anything to ignite a conversation.

People will respond positively to you when their needs are being met. Everyone wants to be appreciated, accepted and affirmed. With-out these three ingredients in your relation-ships, you're pouring water into a basket.

Love the new you

Only you can decide the direction of your life, by what you love and how you love. 1 John 4:28 says "God is Love." Love attracts, it has substance, it's real, it's a feeling, it illuminates, it conquers, it grows, and it can set the world on fire. With the acquiring of this universal quality you would realize that you were made to love.

No longer will your life be lived as unloved, but you have so much love you can not wait to give it away. And the measure you give is the measure you'll receive. You can never out-give your source. You will have no problem applying love in every area of your life. You will be loved because you are a loving person - your transformation has occurred.

FORGET-ME-NOTS

- You can never out-give your source.
- Only you can decide the direction of your life, by what you love and how you love.
- Everyone wants to be appreciated, accepted and affirmed.
- People will respond positively to you when their needs are being met.
- Loving YOU start with your self-confidence: that deep down feeling inside of you that lets you know that you have value.
- A person's five closest friends say a lot about them and where they are heading whether uphill or downhill.
- Love begins, or should begin at home.
- Genuine friendship is at the root of all long lasting relationships.
- Love will cause one to go to other limits as in the case of Alfredo and Juliet, according to Shakespeare.

2

The Priority Factor

Many people miss out on one of the surest ways to add major blessings to their life. They either do not know about it or fail to embrace the concept. "But seek ye first the kingdom of God, and his righteousness; and all these things shall be added unto you." (Matthew 6:33 KJV) How can you miss?

I love music, especially the sound of a great orchestra. It lifts my spirit and puts me in another world. Music is sometimes classified as the "food of love" because it has the tendency to soothe the heart and soul and connects people universally. You will find however, that in order for an orchestra to produce great music, all of its instruments need to perform in harmony or in other words they need to be in alignment or in concert with each other. Then what you hear is so in sync, it lifts your spirit, your heart and soul as it does mine.

As human beings, our life gets out of balance when our priorities are out of whack. Just like a swerving car in need of a wheel alignment. Relief returns when we get back in sync. In order to keep spreading love it's important that you align yourself properly; you cannot distribute effectively if you're not plugged in to the source.

Priority # 1

God wants firsts: first love, first thoughts, first words, first fruits and first offerings. He says "Thou shalt not make unto thee any graven image, or any likeness of any thing that is in heaven above, or that is in the earth beneath, or that is in the water under the earth. Thou shalt not bow down thyself to them, nor serve them: for I the LORD thy God am a jealous God, visiting the iniquity of the fathers upon the children unto the third and fourth generation of them that hate me; And shewing mercy unto thousands of them that love me, and keep my commandments" (Ex. 20:4-6 KJV) That means he's not interested in playing second fiddle. He owns everything; he's in control. Pretty serious, don't you think?

I'm always amazed whenever I hear stories of people who give most of their income to God's cause and live off the balance. That to me is love on a higher level.

Some are known to give upwards of 90% annually. "Bring ye all the tithes into the storehouse, that there may be meat in mine house, and prove me now herewith, saith the LORD of hosts, if I will not open you the windows of heaven, and pour you out a blessing, that there shall not be room enough to receive it." (Malachi 3:10 KJV) The tithe is only one tenth, yet they're comfortable giving above and beyond.

Robert G. LeTournea, met his wife when she was twelve and he was in his twenties. She fell in love instantly and began to pray "Oh God, please have him wait for me." He did. Life grew tough for the young couple; at 30 he was unemployed, had a family to support and $5,000 in debt. At times they lacked basic necessities including the absence of running water for several years. In 1919, after the death of their first son, they were forced to prioritize their life by committing themselves to God and began to tithe.

By 1920 LeTournea opened his first garage. The year of the stock market crash he formed his Peoria earth-moving business. Despite the times, he succeeded.

He soon became the greatest obstacle-mover in history, building huge earth-moving machines. During World War II he produced 70% of all the army's earth-moving machinery. God was known as the Chairman of his Board. A lay pastor in the Christian and Missionary Alliance, Robert shared his faith with millions during his life. Additionally he started two agricultural missions in Liberia and established the LeTourneau foundation to channel 90% of his personal salary to Christian endeavors, especially the training of Christian workers in practical skills (such as house-building) which are needed on mission fields. In 1932 he formed a partnership with God and resolved to pledge all his future profits and much of his energy to religion.

"The more time I spent in serving God," he once said, "the more business grew . . . Amen, Brother."[1] And when asked about his views on money he said "I put my own confidence in God. I don't know what the future holds, but I do know Who holds the future. If he wants you to make money to serve His purposes, you'll make it. If he doesn't want you to have money, he'll find ways to take it from you, no matter how much you have."[2]

It takes a heart filled with love to give when there is very little to give. But God loves a cheerful giver and rewards us abundantly when he is honored with our first fruits.

At a very early age I witness my Mom sow into the kingdom by giving of her tithes and offerings. To her as a disciplinarian it was a prerequisite. I am glad that she did, not only was she blessed for doing so but I understood the importance of making God a priority early in life. Learning that He's always there and ready to help no matter what I'm going through. **Where others see an adversity, they are so wrong for it always turns out as a blessing in disguise.** God has a way of breaking man made rules to bless us.

To love God means to serve him in spirit and in truth and to love others as we love our-selves.

A God given dream

A young dreamer one day told his brothers about his dreams including one he had in which they bowed down to him with faces almost touching the ground. They despised him and eventually sold him into slavery.

The slave master who purchased him soon realized that the Lord was blessing this slave beyond measure and promoted him, putting him in charge of his household. That home prospered even more. As a result he was trusted with more responsibility and put in charge of every thing that his master had. This handsome man was well built and while his master was away, his master's wife noticed him and said to him "come to bed with me!" But he refused. She pleaded with him daily but still he refused. He finally fled the house leaving his coat in her hand. She not only fabricated the story to the other servants but also to her husband as soon as he came home. The young man, Joseph, was imprisoned. Again the Lord favored him and he was put in charge of the prisoners by the warden. The King, Pharaoh, dreamt several dreams that troubled him. No one in the land was able to interpret the King's dreams. But because of Joseph's familiarity with dreams and making the Lord a priority in his life, he was sought out and brought in to the king to render interpretations. He accomplished the task, revealing to the King that a famine was beckoning. Joseph was put in charge of famine operations.

The famine intensified, affecting his family in another area. So, ten of his brothers journeyed to Egypt in order to buy food. They unknowingly encountered their brother Joseph, the man in charge. They all bowed down to him prior to making their purchase. As a result of this reunion, Joseph's entire family were brought to and dwelt in Egypt. (Gen. 37, 39, 40, 41, 42) Putting the Lord first paid huge dividends for Joseph.

Throughout history, the people who put God first in their lives always seem to be blessed beyond measure. They are plugged directly into that source of endless, unconditional, inescapable love and therefore freely and compassionately dole it out to others. And his rich blessings overshadow them.

Priority # 2

If you are married your spouse is to be loved second to your creator, followed by your kids.

"Wherefore they are no more twain, but one flesh. What therefore God hath joined together, let not man put asunder." (Matthew 19:6 KJV) During courtship very careful attention is paid to the pleasing of each other. The wooer researches in an effort solely to please. In his book *Letters to Karen* Charlie W. Shedd writes: "It is a wise couple who continue this expression of their love into marriage and even increase it as the years pass."[3] Shedd further states, "Three words describe many a marriage- 'They quit courting.'"[4]

I have seen couples who make the foolish mistake of placing their kids or the cat, dog and others above their spouse. They walk the dog but fail to take frequent walks with each other. They spend quality time with others and miss quality time with their spouse. As a result, the home's in chaos; there's no harmony, love fades, and dies eventually, sending them to divorce court, very catastrophic - the orchestra flops - the music becomes a blob.

I have also noticed that when there is proper alignment in the home, unity, trust, communication, confidence, blessings and commitment are some of its by-products.

Priority # 3

The job helps to create harmony. It provides for the needs of the family and grows God's kingdom. I believe that you should be the best that you can be on your job by going the extra mile so that when you leave you would have kept your love alive in your co-workers hearts.

If you are a self-employed, passion and purpose should go into everything that you do so that your legacy would be one to be reckoned with. William Danforth challenges in his book *I Dare You*: "Are you content to have posterity look at your life so far and say, 'That is all he was capable of?' Or are you one of the priceless few, one of those with a restless feeling that someday you are going to climb to your rightful place of leadership? That someday you are going to create something worthy of your best?"[5]

Priority # 4

John F. Kennedy declared, "Ask not what your country can do for you, but what you can do for your country."[6] Martin Luther King Jr. said "I have a dream."[7] Winston Churchill challenged, "Never in the field of human conflict was so much owed by so many to so few."[8] Abraham Lincoln who failed over and over again had this to say: "We have nothing to fear but fear itself."[9] What are you willing to give back to the country which offered you the opportunity to become who you are?

America remains the greatest country in the world. Yet so many Americans take their heritage for granted. They do not value their freedom. So many were born with a gold spoon in their mouth, therefore it takes them traveling to other countries before they realize what they have.

We find that people risk their lives everyday to get here, yet no one is trying to leave; it provides equal opportunity for everyone. "To whom much is given much is expected" Is a famous maxim. We find that the most valuable things we have are those which come easy to us and cost us nothing. Yet we are able to touch others in a special way when we spread some love on others.

Giving and receiving

I launched a smile, far out it sailed
on life's troubled sea,
And many more than I could
count came sailing back
to me.

I clasped a hand while whispering,
"The clouds will melt away."
I felt my life was very blessed All
through the hours that day.

I sent a thought of happiness
Where it was needed sore,
And very soon thereafter, found

Joy adding to my store.
I wisely shared my slender hoard,
Toil-earned coins of gold;
But presently it flowed right
back. Increased a hundredfold.

I helped another climb a hill,
A little thing to do:
And yet it brought a rich reward,
A friendship that was new.

I think each morning when I rise,
Of how I may achieve,
I know by serving I advance,

By giving I receive.[10]

- *Thomas Gaines*

FORGET-ME-NOTS

- To whom much is given much is expected.

- What are you willing to give back to the country which offered you the opportunity to become who you are?

- Passion and purpose should go into everything that you do.

- Be the best that you can be on your job by going the extra mile.

- When there's proper alignment in the home, unity, trust, communication, confidence, blessings and commitment are some of the by-products.

- It takes a heart filled with love to give when there is very little to give.

- To love God means to serve him in spirit and in truth and to love our neighbor as ourselves.

- As human beings, our life gets out of balance when our priorities are out of whack.

"There
is nothing wrong or disgraceful
about getting knocked down.
Virtually all the greats have
experienced temporary defeats.
Those are the learning times,
the opportunities for you to
grow and achieve your
destiny."[1]

-Skip Ross

3

The Commitment Factor

Professor John Powell in his book *The Secret of Staying in Love writes:* "The commitment of love, at whatever level, has to be a permanent thing, a life wager. If I say I am your friend, I will always be your friend, not as long as or until anything. I will always be there for you. Effective love is not like the retractable point on a ballpoint pen. If I say I am your man I will always be your man."[2]

If there's no commitment between two people whether in thought, word or action love's forced to sit on the fence. The match and the coal have to agree in order for the coal to burn. It's a known fact that if you want the fireplace to give you heat, you have got to keep feeding it some wood. The German Philosopher Goethe said: "Until one is committed, there is hesitance, the chance to draw back. Always ineffectiveness. Concerning all acts of initiative (and creation), there is one elemental truth the ignorance of which kills countless ideas and splendid plans; that the moment one commits oneself, then providence moves too. All sorts of things occur to help one that would never have otherwise occurred. A whole stream of events issues from the decision, raising in one's favor all manner of unforeseen incidents and meetings and material assistance which no man could have dreamed would come his way. Whatever you can do or dream you can begin it. Genius has boldness and power and magic in it. Begin now."[3]

So many people find it hard to commit to something and end up falling for anything. It is startling but our society is filled with people who spend most of their life sitting on the fence. They are afraid of what others will think or say if the were to make a decision to live a *love is forever* life, afraid to leave their nest or what some may call their comfort zone. With commitment to love - comes decisions. Consequently, decisions to fulfill one another's needs. Even if these needs keep on changing, as we grow we change, so does our needs and the needs of the one loved. To look for and fulfill one's changing needs a relationship is all about spreading love on in layers.

Commitment inspires growth

In 2002 after my divorce I committed myself to relational personal growth. I had realized that the more I grow and improve, the better able I am to help others. Previously I had thought that my spouse was to blame for the demise of our relationship. But a relationship is like a coin; there are two sides. Though I failed, failure was not going to be attached to me. My search for materials on phenomenal relation-ships skyrocketed.

A few years later I met Pastors Philip and Holly Wagner at Oasis Christian Center. At the time they had been married for almost 2 decades and continued to enjoy a growing relationship. Their seminar on relationship sustained the foundation to my recovery. In addition, I continually read books, attend conferences, listen to audio messages and learn from some of the best on the subject.

Being empowered, my obligation is to give back to young people looking for love in all the wrong faces and all the wrong places, to adults with failed relationship after relationship and to a world filled with envy and hatred.

Commitment needs a vision

Oftentimes I have seen individuals loaded with potential who fail to grasp a leader's vision. Fear of commitment is one of the main causes of the lazy man's disease "fence sitting." Lack of commitment in any relationship could be attributed to the inability to tie into the vision of the counterpart.

When people jump on board a leader's vision then momentum emerges and the organization becomes unstoppable. There seems to be some-thing extra that radiates from someone once they commit, it is like the glue that bonds that entity together, creating such synergy within the group. This in turn makes it easier to turn the vision into reality. Now, you may question: What does commitment have to do with love? In life when we're interested in something we tend to do it when it is convenient but when we are committed, we do it no matter what stands in our way.

Author Berton Braley had this to say: "If you want a thing bad enough to go out and fight for it, to work day and night for it, to give up your time, and your sleep for it...if all that you dream and scheme is about it, and life seems useless and worthless without it...if you gladly sweat for it and fret for it and plan for it and lose all you terror of opposition for it...if you simply go after that thing you want with all of your capacity, strength and sagacity, faith, hope and confidence and stern pertinacity…if neither cold, poverty, famine, nor gout, sick-ness nor pain, of body and brain, can keep you away from the thing that you want…if dogged and grim you beseech it, with the help of God, you WILL get it!"[4]

Every relationship needs commitment in it in order for it to grow and when the focus is love, we raise our standards - experiencing a higher and deeper love. Without love in a relationship there is no momentum and without moment-um, there is no progress.

Committed to a cause

She was referred to as "Moses" not only by the hundreds of slaves she helped to freedom but also by the thousands of others she inspired. Because of her commitment to a cause Harriet Tubman became the most famous leader of the Underground Railroad to aid slaves escaping the Free states or Canada.

Born into slavery in Maryland, she escaped her own chains in 1849 to safety in Pennsylvania. A feat accomplished through the Underground Railroad, an elaborate and secret series of houses, tunnels, and roads set up by abolitionists and former slaves. "When I found I had crossed the [Mason-Dixon] line, I looked at my hands to see if I were the same person,"

Tubman later wrote. ". . . the sun came like gold through the tree and over the field and I felt like I was in heaven." She would spend the rest of her life helping other slaves escape to freedom.

After her escape, she worked as a maid in Philadelphia and joined the large and active abolitionist group in the city. In 1850, after Congress passed the Fugitive Slave Act, making it illegal to help a runaway slave, Tubman decided to join the Underground Railroad.

Her first expedition took place in 1851, when she managed to thread her way through the backwoods to Baltimore and return to the North with her sister and her sister's children. From that time until the onset of the Civil War, she traveled to the South about 18 times and helped close to 300 slaves escape. In 1857, led her parents to freedom in Auburn, New York, and resided there.

Tubman was never caught and never lost a slave to the Southern militia. As her reputation grew, so too did the desire among Southerners to put a stop to her activities. Rewards for her capture once totaled about $40,000, a lot of money in those days. During the Civil War, Tubman served as a nurse, scout, and sometime-spy for the Union army, mainly in South Carolina. She also took part in a military campaign that resulted in the rescue of 756 slaves and destroyed millions of dollars' worth of enemy property.

After the war, Tubman returned to Auburn and continued her involvement in social issues, including the women's rights movement. In 1908, she established a home in Auburn for elderly and indigent blacks that later became known as the Harriet Tubman Home. She died on March 10, 1913, at approximately age of 93.[5]

Tubman's passionate commitment of love for her people kept her going back until every slave was freed, regardless of the dangers involved.

Childhood commitment

"When I was a child, I spake as a child I understood as a child, I thought as a child: but when I became a man, I put away childish things." (I Cor. 13: 11 KJV)

When I was only nine years of age I committed my life to my Maker. My desire to serve Him in spirit and truth was paramount. **During those pre-teen years my dedication to what He wanted of me took center stage in my life.** My recollection goes back to when I would read and discuss verses of scripture with senior members of our church congregation. At times some of my favorite sermons were delivered from the pulpit. I tithed diligently. My commitment to God's cause was real; my relationship was like an ebbing tide. I believed that He loved me and wanted the best from me. My parents envisioned this and supported me by sending me to a Christian High School instead of a government operated one. But somewhere along the way during my late teens there was a shift. I took a leave of absence. As a result, I fell off the horse.

Getting back on the horse

"What do you do when you fall off the horse?" I have used this question like a broken record with my three sons who are 9, 10 and 12, whenever they fail to accomplish their best. Falling off the horse could be a tragedy if one lacks the determination to get back on.

In 2002 after the fall and being kicked around by the horse, I decided that it was time to get back on and ride.

Alfredo and I met at an acting class. He was at the time going through a divorce and com-muted from Las Vegas to L.A. with his 4 and 6 year old sons, in a search for modeling opportunities to support them. While recovering from the ailments of my divorce, he found me as a sounding board. As a result we bonded and became roommates.

Alfredo was already attending church at the Oasis in Los Angeles and one Sunday he invited me. He said "John, their praise and worship is off the chain." I showed up and found it to be true. Thanks to my roommate Alfredo, I became planted and positively turned my life around. To me it has become a love thing.

Staying in love takes work, much more than many are prepared for. If a person is not willing to work on him or herself they should stay out of the falling in love business. The world is full of too many abandoned relation-ships and broken hearts.

DON'T QUIT

When things go wrong, as they
sometimes will,
When the road you're trudging seems
all uphill,
When the funds are low and the debts
are high,
And you want to smile, but you have to
sigh,
When care is pressing you down a bit,
Rest, if you must-but don't you quit.

Life is queer with its twists and turns,
As everyone of us sometimes learns,
And many a failure turns about
When he might have won had he stuck
it out;

Don't give up though the pace seems slow-
You might succeed with another blow.

Often the goal is nearer than
It seems to a faint and faltering man,
Often the struggler has given up
When he might have captured the victor's cup.
And learned too late, when the night slipped down,
How close he was to the victor's crown.

Success is failure turned inside out-
The silver tint of the clouds of doubt-
And you never can tell how close you are,
It might be near when it seems afar;
So stick to the fight when you're hardest hit-
Its when things seems worst that you mustn't quit.[6]

- Unknown

FORGET-ME-NOTS

- Staying in love takes work, much more than many are prepared for.

- If a person is not willing to work on him or herself they should stay out of the falling in love business. The world is full of too many abandoned relation-ships and broken hearts.

- Every relationship needs commitment in it in order for it to grow and when the focus is love, we raise our standards – experiencing a higher and deeper love.

- Without love in a relationship there is no momentum and without momentum, there is no progress.

- In life when we're interested in something we tend to do it when it is convenient but when we are committed, we do it no matter what stands in our way.

- When you fall off the horse, get up, get back on and ride to the finish line.

- An adult-like commitment carries more significance than a childlike commitment.

- There seems to be something extra that radiates from someone once they commit, it is like the glue that bonds that entity together, creating such synergy within the group.

- When people jump on board a leader's vision then momentum emerges and the organization becomes unstoppable.

- If there's no commitment between two people whether in thought, word or action love's forced to sit on the fence.

- It's a known fact that if you want the fireplace to give you heat, you have got to keep feeding it some wood.

"Respect involves an appraisal of ourselves first, and then others."[2]

-Duane Hodgin.

4

The Respect Factor

Dr. Emerson Eggerichs states in his book *Love & Respect:* "When you love or respect unconditionally, you are following God and his will for you."[2] I Peter 3:9 NIRV reads: "Don't pay back unkind words with unkind words. Instead, pay them back with kind words" and Ephesians 6:7-8 NIV reads:" Serve wholeheartedly, as if you were serving the Lord, not men, because you know that the Lord will reward everyone for whatever good he does, whether he is slave or free." Respect is like a two way street. Respect and you will be respected.

Falling out of love

People who fall out of love with themselves do so by first losing their self-respect. "Self-respect is like weaving a coat of armor that no one can cut through,"[3] according to Henry Wadsworth Longfellow.

In any relationship, once lack of respect for self or the other party surfaces and is not soon fixed that relationship drastically slides down-hill catapulting into fallout, "like a stitch in time saves nine."

According to Dr. Eggerichhs, one of the questions women who are married frequently ask is, "How can I get my husband to love me as much as I love him?"[4] Men thrive on being respected. "Wives do not need a lot of coaching on being loving. It is something God built into them, and they do it naturally. However, they do need help with respect,"[5] states Dr. Eggerichs.

I believe that lack of respect is the number one symptom and cause of divorce. The words: I was wrong, I'm sorry and I apologize, could be the three most important phrases in any relationship in addition to I love you. Without their proper, frequent usage that relationship will easily collapse. It is a known fact that spouses who do not respect each other, compounded over time are en-route to the divorce courts before long.

Where does disrespect begin?

So many parents are afraid to draw the line in the sand when kids overstep their boundary and lose respect. These same kids, if not disciplined, grow up as menace to society, if not retrained in the areas of love and respect. Most young women are raised in homes where the dad is not respected by mom, so they tend to adopt the same philosophy and bring it into their marriage.

The people in our world who find themselves having no respect for the law usually wind up behind bars, while those who ignore the law written by God's own hands always seem to suffer the consequences. As most parents tell their kids: "If you play with fire you will get burned." Does it imply that if one should choose to disrespect another that they are playing with fire in that relationship? What do you think? As I stated in my book *The 5 Steps To Changing Your Life*, if one were to jump of the top of a tall building inevitably they are going to fall.

What men really want

Outside of inviting sexual love a man needs approval and respect.

If you would like to be respected it is imperative that you first show respect for others. So many married men desperately crave respect from their wives. On the other hand women find it hard to respect men if they feel that he has not done enough to make her happy. They fail to realize that happiness, like success, is a journey. It is like saying "fireplace give me some heat and then I'll give the wood."

Men are meant to be leaders. Therefore they want to be respected. And when they do not get it, the relationship suffers. As a woman is moved by a man who tells her daily that he loves her, so is a man moved by a woman who tells him that she respects him. The woman who delights in belittling her husband by calling him names is gradually creating havoc in her marriage and paving the road to the divorce court.

"The woman absolutely needs love, and the man absolutely needs respect. It's as simple-and as difficult as that."[6] And "Every action in the company of others ought to be done with some sign of respect to those present."[7] George Washington.

FORGET-ME-NOTS

- As a woman is moved by a man who tells her daily that he loves her, so is a man moved by a woman who tells him that she respects him.

- Men are meant to be leaders; therefore they want to be respected.

- If you would like to be respected it is imperative that you first show respect for others.

- Outside of inviting sexual love a man needs approval and respect.

- If one were to jump of the top of a tall building inevitably they're going to fall.

- It is a known fact that spouses who do not respect each other, compounded over time are en-route to the divorce courts before long.

- The people who fall out of love with themselves do so by first losing their self-respect.

- The words: I was wrong, I'm sorry and I apologize, could be the three most important phrases in any relationship in addition to I love you.

- Respect is like a two way street. Respect and you'll be respected.

Let it be instilled in your mindset that your best is still to come…

"I can live for two months on a good compliment"[1]

- Mark Twain

5

The Affirmation Factor

When we affirm someone we tend to lift their spirits, and we all know that a fulfilled person is more likely to spread happiness than an unhappy person. By doing so our good deed gets multiplied instantly. Goethe states: "Treat a man as he appears to be and you make him worse. But treat a man as if he already were what he potentially could be, and you make him what he should be."[2] There is tremendous value in each of us and when someone else sees it and helps us to see it we are elevated to higher heights on the love quotient. Thus our love for self, for others and our world increases. Elbert Hubbard said, "There is something that is much more scarce, some-thing finer far, something rarer than ability. It is the ability to recognize ability."

Add value to others

A little over five years ago when I embarked upon my writing career, my friend Mr. Y. told me that I had it within me and I should go for it. Imagine me, a high school dropout, lack of eloquence, no typing skills and deficient in other skills, rising to the occasion to write screenplays, and now books. Not only did he lift my spirits by telling me that I could do it but he cared enough to let me know that he believed in me. Affirming someone by telling them know that you believe in them, will gain you points almost as valuable as saying "I'm sorry, I was wrong and I apologize" would.

What women really want

A few years ago, I met a young woman in our church, let's call her Ms. A. She possesses a tremendous gift of speaking, eloquently delivering the word. In addition to her talent she has a physical and spiritual beauty that radiates from the inside out. I noticed that the upkeep of her hair was far behind everything else that she had going for her. See, as a kid growing up in a home with five sisters back in the islands, I saw my mom at work with her girls. Her weekly advice to them was "girls get your hair done, remember your hair beautifies you." One day I had someone deliver a gift certificate to Ms. A. for a full session at a hair salon. She reluctantly accepted. Since then I've seen her gradually transformed into a beauty queen.

In marriage, a lot of men miss out on the opportunity to lift a woman to another level by not being watchful, observant and heedful to that woman's needs. "It is indispensable for a woman to know that her husband is aware of her as a person. His thoughtful attention to her comfort is a visible demonstration to her of his love. It provides further a unifying bond between them, for as a man shows his thoughtful concern for his wife, she blossoms as a flower in the sun while he feels an expansion of his better self through remembering her,"[3] writes: Dr. Aubrey Andelin in his book *Man of Steel and Velvet.*

LITTLE THINGS MEAN A LOT

Blow me a kiss from across the room,
Say I look nice, when I'm not.
Touch my hair as you pass my chair,
Little things mean a lot.
Give me your arm as we cross the street,
Call me at six on the dot.
A line a day when you're far away,
Little things mean a lot.

You don't have to buy me diamonds and pearls,

Champagne, sables or such,
I never cared much for diamonds and pearls,
For honestly, honey, they just cost money.

Give me your hand when I've lost the way,
Give me a shoulder to cry on.
Whether the day is bright or gray,
Give me your heart to rely on.
Give me the warmth of a secret smile,
To show you haven't forgot.
For now and forever, for always and ever.
Little things mean a lot.[4]

Compliment others

One of the surest ways to break the ice with a new person is to pay them a sincere compliment. When you compliment someone you add to their value but when you do it behind their backs you multiply their value. Some husbands miss the boat by failing to compliment their spouse regularly. We'll get into this later but a sincere compliment returns big dividends.

Most people are so focused on themselves they have no time left to focus on others. By letting these grand opportunities pass by, they fail to develop a new relationship or enhance an existing one. "Take a lesson from the flowers. They know how to attract the bee. But instead of scolding or coercing, the flower just puts out a few drops of nectar. The flower knows that the bee is hungry for nectar. It provides food to feed that hunger"[5] states Les Giblin in his book *How To Have Power and Confidence In Dealing With People.*

Edifying others

A person who spreads love edifies and not de-edifies. The people who engage in tearing others down are missing the boat filled with love and overflowing - they spread poison.
John Maxwell in his book *25 Ways to Win With People* states, "Many of us desire to win so much that we forget what it takes to get there"[6]

Maxwell also tells a story about Lou Whittaker who was a mountain climber. In 1984, Whittaker led the first all-American team to the top of Mt. Everest. The final campsite at twenty-seven thousand feet was finally reached by five members of the team after months of demanding effort. They met in a crowded tent with only two thousand feet to go.

Whittaker had a tough decision to make knowing how highly the five climbers were to stand on the highest peak on earth. But two of them would have to go back to the previous camp, get food supplies and oxygen, and then return to the camp where they now met. Upon completion of this assignment these two climbers would be in no condition to go for the summit. The other climbers would stay in the tent that day to drink water, breathe oxygen, and rest, to prepare for the climb the following day. The first decision Whittaker made was to stay at the final campsite to coordinate the team's activities. The second, to send the two strongest climbers down the mountain to get the supplies. The two weaker climbers would rest, renew their strength and receive the glory of the summit.

When asked why he didn't assign himself the summit run, he said, "my job was to put other people on top."[7]

Whittaker understood the double win effect in a winning. As the saying goes, "You win when you help others win."

Appreciate others

Accepting people and embracing their differences is the key to every new relationship. Sydney J. Harris states, "People want to be appreciated, not impressed. They want to be regarded as human beings, not as mere sounding boards for other people's egos. They want to be treated as an end in themselves, not as a means toward the gratification of another's vanity."[8]

We cannot change people, only ourselves, they've got to want to change and embrace it. One psychologist expressed: "No one has the power to reform another person, but by liking the other person as he is, you give him the power to change himself."[9]

Feed their hunger

Many women fail to realize the impact they have on their husbands if they accept and appreciate him to the fullest. Men tend to perform at their best when there is stability in their love life - true acceptance from their spouse. Wives nag and complain, thinking that should get the man's attention and him sharpen up. It does not work; Men excel because they're approved. The president of one corporation expressed it this way: "When a wife accepts her husband and gives him the feeling that she is pleased with him, as he is, it is like getting a shot of self confidence in the arm every time the husband goes home. He says to himself, "if she likes me, maybe I'm not such a bad guy after all,' He goes out to meet the world the next morning brimming over with self-confidence and with a feeling that whatever comes along, he can lick it. But when a man goes home to a nagging, complaining, scolding wife, it's like having all the fight taken out of them. Her continual dissatisfaction with him comes across to him and adds to his germs of self-doubt. He begins to doubt himself."[10]

Failure to recognize another human being is by far one of the greatest tragedies in relation-ships. Soldiers die for it and babies cry for it. Every one wants to be accepted. Les Giblin states, "Acceptance is a vitamin. We all hunger to be accepted as we are. Someone we can let our hair down and take our shoes off with."[11] He also states, "You can't make the other fellow feel important in your presence if you secretly feel that he is a nobody."[12]

I love my church Oasis Christian Center. It is like the United Nations – so diverse in culture. It is a great place to see unity in action despite its diversity. We live in a society in which people find it difficult to get along with others. We see it in police profiling, riots, school violence, and the place where it should not, but all begins – the home.

The civil rights revolution of the sixties has somewhat changed the shape of America when it comes to racial tension but a lot of mending still needs to be accomplished. Mainly because love in the heart and home continues to decline; throwing venomous teenagers out into our schools and eventually our workplace and the rest of society. 'Psychologists, criminologists, ministers, and now even doctors tell us that most of the trouble in this world is caused by unhappy people.'[13] While "Criminologists say that many crimes, especially sensational ones, are performed by people who never had satisfied their craving for being noticed"[14] states Les Giblin.

Affirmation, Attention and Acceptance places value on others. Give them away and your love will not be forgotten even after you are gone. It would be like casting your bread upon the waters, and returning to you after many days.

FORGET-ME-NOTS

- Affirmation, Attention and Acceptance places value on others.

- Failure to recognize another human being is by far one of the greatest tragedies in relationships.

- We cannot change people, only ourselves, they have got to want to change and embrace it.

- Accepting people and embracing their differences is the key to every new relationship.

- A person who spreads love edifies and not de-edifies.

- There is magic in complimenting people in front of other people and behind their backs.

- Affirming someone by telling them that you believe in them, will gain you points close to *I'm sorry, I was wrong and I apologize*.

- When we affirm someone we tend to lift their spirits, and we all know that a fulfilled person is more likely to spread happiness than an unhappy person.

"Among those emotional needs, none is more basic than the need for love and affection, the need to sense that he or she belongs and is wanted." [1]

- Gary Chapman

6

The Communication Factor

Ralph Waldo Emerson says: "What you do speaks so loudly that I cannot hear what you say."[2] In my opinion two thirds of the worlds' problems could be solved through effective communication and the other third one through empathy. Most marriage counselors will tell you that lack of effective communication brings most couples into their offices and next to it is not the lack of money but the failure to walk in the other spouse's moccasin for a while. So, if that is the case why do so many fail to effectively communicate? This chapter in the spread some love quotient, may not be a quick fix but if applied could help to heal the fracture in most existing marriages, and give direction to those wanting to take up the mantle of marriage and run with it.

Put your heart into it

It is important to lend an ear when you listen, but do we really hear what the other person is saying? Any well trained actor will tell you that the words do not matter so much as what is said underneath the words - the subtext. They listen for what is under the text in order to determine their response. If you were to watch a great movie with great dialog in it, you would tend to get more from the actor who is listening and reacting, than from the one talking in the scene. The lips move but what does their heart or their feelings say? Communication plays a major role in how we love; it is of utmost importance to the other party that they know what you say and how you feel so they like an actor in the role can give the correct response.

Listening is an art. Men usually say what needs to be said and get it over with. While on the other hand a woman may not have anything important to say at times, she may just want a listening ear. Other times she may not need for the man to solve a problem for her, sometimes she just wants him to hear the problem. A smart man if not sure, will in humility ask her if she just wants him to learn about the situation or need some help in solving the problem. She will tell him happily but most of all she would realize that he was listening to her with all his heart. "When we listen for genuine understanding, we are no longer 'playing the role' of listening, but we are finally in the moment, and the person knows it."[3] writes Les Parrott.

Undivided attention

This is a very effective form of communication. It helps to create synergy in dialog - finishing the sentence for the other party. Have you ever seen a couple sitting on the couch, the TV turned off, and they are talking to each other not missing a single word or holding each other's hand on a walking date or dining together where the food is secondary because they are completely absorbed in each other. It kind of makes you wish you were cast in the role. It is sad to see though, that as most of these relationships mature these same couples have very little to share with each other. They act as if everything about each other has already been told or discovered. Their creativity during courtship is now in the ice box - frozen. The light of love should never be put out or allowed to die in the heart of the one you love.

Here are some ways to step up communication in a relationship.

1. Doing chores together.
2. Go out at least once a week.
3. Possess a forgiving attitude.
4. Welcome mystery; you do not have to know everything.
5. Become good at talking things over.

Women thrive on masculine approval - they come alive when exposed to it like my friends' plant did once it was placed outdoors. The best way for a woman to know that you approve of her is for you to tell her so. Most husbands fail at this miserably. A husband should aim to daily compliment his wife, do something nice for her and tell her that he loves her. If she gets a lovely idea of herself, she will try to become it.

A smart husband will give his wife pleasant things to think on while he's away. This will take his love life to another level by pouring honey on her thoughts (of him) not only when he is away but later when in bed with her.

FORGET-ME-NOTS

- A smart husband will give his wife pleasant things to think on.

- Women thrive on masculine approval.

- The best way for a woman to know that you approve of her is for you to tell her so.
- The light of love should never be put out or allowed to die in the heart of the one you love.

- Communication plays a major role in how we love; it is of utmost importance to the other party that they know what you say and how you feel so they like an actor in the role can give the correct response.

- Two thirds of the worlds' problems could be solved through effective communication.

"The best things in life are never rationed. Friendship, loyalty, love do not require coupons."[1]

- George T. Hewitt

7

The Loyalty Factor

A few weeks after meeting Mr. Y for the first time, I was introduced to his friend Carl. They attended the same college, worked and hung out together for decades. When Mr. Y. was going through his divorce in the 90s, they became roommates. A few years ago I worked as an actor on one of Mr. Y's movies. That year he produced 4 films, one in Canada and 3 in the US. He was swamped, so he asked Carl to help on this project that I worked on. Carl produced that movie as if it was his own film. Today, not only has he moved into Mr. Y's office but has been put in charge of development on all of his major films. I have seen their friendship grow strong through the years, so much that Mr. Y's son calls him Uncle Carl.

Indispensable bond

"And Ruth said, Entreat me not to leave thee, or to return from following after thee: for whither thou goest, I will go; and where thou lodgest, I will lodge: thy people shall be my people, and thy God my God: Where thou diest, will I die, and there will I be buried: the LORD do so to me, and more also, [if ought] but death part thee and me." (Ruth 1:16-17 KJV)

Ruth, a Maobite woman and daughter-in-law of the widowed Naomi became widowed. Naomi, along with her two daughter-in-laws Oprah and Ruth traveled to Judah; the home of the two women.

Expressing her gratitude, Naomi encouraged them to stay behind but they resented; prefer-ring to travel on with her. Naomi pleaded with them, reminding them that she was old and had no plans of getting remarried, and even if she did, and had two sons in the process, her sons would be too young to marry any of the two women. The women wept and Oprah decided to leave but Ruth clung to Naomi refusing to return with her sister-in-law. Ruth had developed a bond with Naomi that was so inseparable.

Some people fall in love and the first words out of their mouths are:

1. I will love you forever.
2. I want to spend my life with you.
3. You mean everything to me.
4. For you I will do anything.
5. You can have everything I have.
6. I want to spend all my time with you.
7. You make me who I am.
8. You will always be all that I ever need or want.
9. I'm stuck on you with crazy glue.
10. I'm always thinking about you.
11. There's no me without you babe.

And when the first obstacle occurs, they want to throw in the towel stating:
"It's done.
We're not meant for each other.
I can't stand you."
They do not realize that the obstacle could be the magical turn which produces growth in that relationship. Imagine an action thriller or love drama movie without twists and turns in it, a basketball game when every shot goes inside the basket, a relationship without any testing.

Some would say "if you love me prove it" and the lover will prove sexually how strong their love is for that demanding partner. On the other hand, when the challenges present them-selves in that relationship, when it is time for the proof of love, many call it quits. "Welcome to the real world of marriage, where hairs are always on the sink and little white spots cover the mirror, where arguments center on which way the toilet paper comes off and whether the lid should be up or down. It's a world where shoes do not walk to the closet and drawers do not close themselves, where coats do not like hangers and socks go AWOL during laundry. In this world, a look can hurt and a word can crush. Intimate lovers can become enemies, and marriage a battlefield."2 states Gary Chapman.

The down times

The real you always surface when your back is up against the wall. What you are made of steps right onto center stage, and loyalty in who you are and what you believe becomes magnified. Jesus said "If ye love me, keep my commandments." (John 14:15 KJV) Prove love, how much you love me your actions will show, even when the chips are down and nothing seems to be going right in the relationship.

A growing relationship is somewhat like the life of a butterfly. First, it is like a baby caterpillar; nice and green having a blast, eating all it can, enjoying the good times. Then a cocoon forms around it. Inside, this insect twists and turns, and eventually emerges as a beautiful butterfly. Without the change there will be no growth and without the growth there is no change. What if someone were to try to pry open the cocoon and set that butterfly free prematurely? If it came out alive, it would, no doubt suffer broken wings and limbs. It would be a "butter-flop" instead of a butterfly; unable to fly.

Jumping ship won't make a person who refuses to accept growth, sometimes disguised as a challenge, change into a better person. Imagine that caterpillar jumping from plant to plant having a blast, refusing to change into a colorful butterfly. The same thing happens when we jump from one relationship to another relationship refusing to fix our problems in order to remain loyal in our existing involvement, we fail to grow.

Loyalty involves continuity

The stream of water keeps on flowing to the ocean consistently - day after day. I have seen young lovers who are all over each other trying to do whatever good deed necessary to acquire each others love, using constant woo tactics. Then the time comes, after they get married, and their honeymoon. Their marriage relationship is at an all time high.

As time drags on, they become more familiar with each others pet peeves. Kids arrive, the nights are long and life becomes a bore. There are no more good times, no more being all over each other, no more makeup in place, no more of: "I can't wait to see you." The life they envisioned seems like it belongs to someone else's; their dreams have now become nightmares. They can only see a breakup coming like a freight train. Their biggest mistake in not keeping it together goes back to this famous statement: "What you did to get them is what you need to do in order to keep them."

Loyalty is trust. The best proof of love is trust. A trusting relationship is a lasting relationship. Without trust, hearts are broken and the bond is severed and turned into another love catastrophe.

FORGET-ME-NOTS

- Loyalty is trust. The best proof of love is trust.

- What you did to get that person is what you need to keep doing in order to keep them.

- Jumping ship will not make a person who refuses to accept growth, disguised as a challenge, change into a better person.

- A growing relationship is somewhat like the life of a butterfly.

- The real you always surface when your back is up against the wall.

*"One
who is humble
may have many virtues
and achievements,
but he realizes his
own weaknesses,
mistakes and
limitations."*[1]

-Aubrey Andelin

8

The Humility Factor

"These six things the LORD hates, Yes, seven are an abomination to Him: A proud look, A lying tongue, Hands that shed innocent blood, A heart that devises wicked plans, Feet that are swift in running to evil, A false witness who speaks lies, And one who sows discord among brethren." (Proverbs 6:16-19 NKJV)

Pride, which is the opposite of humility, is first on the list of the seven things that the Lord hates. When the source of love says he "hates" something it is definitely worth paying attention to. Dr. Aubrey Andelin writes: "Humility is one of the most desirable traits of human personality. No man is truly great without it. It shows for all life and a greatness of spirit. A humble man recognizes himself and others as participants in a divine plan which glorifies the human potential and recognizes that from the most inauspicious beginnings may arise great-ness. Humility adds velvet to a man which tempers the hard steel and balances his self-confidence."2

It is amazing to see what happens when a man who is in the position of leadership chose to listen to the ideas and opinions of those in his care. It not only humbles him but humbles them also in return. The person who thinks that he knows everything and fails to learn from others, is on his way to failure in less time than he can count.

Humility breathes fresh air into a relationship full of give and take An oxygenized association is a healthy one in which the parties concerned know when to listen and when to speak. Have you ever been in the company of others who just dominated every bit of the conversation? And you ask yourself "when are they going to allow me to say something instead of talking forever about themselves?" Yet we still need to love them and give them room to grow.

The famous saying "People make the world go around" has merit. Without each other love is forced to become fixated.

Needing people is a fact but letting them know how much we need them is a requirement. This act of selflessness produces humility in all of our relationships with mankind.

It takes a humble man to say to his wife "I need you" and a humble woman to say "I was wrong, I'm sorry and I apologize." Humility in action puts that relationship on a higher level. "For whosoever exalteth himself shall be abased; and he that humbleth himself shall be exalted." (Luke 14:11 KJV)

FORGET-ME-NOTS

- Humility in action puts the relationship on a higher level.
- Needing people is a fact but letting them know how much we need them is a requirement.
- Humility breathes fresh air into a relationship full of give and take.
- The person who thinks that he knows everything and fails to learn from others, is on his way to failure.
- The person who thinks that he knows everything is on his way to failure.
- It is amazing to see what happens when a man who is in the position of leader-ship chose to listen to the ideas and opinions of those in his care.

***"One
who is youthful
has his mind open to new
ideas."*** [1]

-Dr. Aubrey Andelin

9

The Youthfulness Factor

At least two thirds of my associations fall between the ages of 18 and 30. I love their zest, their vim, their vitality. They not only keep me young but place me on the cutting edge when it comes to my dreams and my productivity, they keep me filled with passion. I must say I am blessed as I do not think it is by accident that I am inking this book today. Association is the key.

I have seen so many married couples who lose their zest, vim and vitality in their relationship right after the honeymoon. Love ends there and it seems like the sexual gratification was all that mattered, as they fail in other ways, mainly re-discovering each other.

Keep the fires burning

Youthfulness in a relationship helps to keep the fires of love burning brightly. Without that element, it would be like a wood stove that has run out of wood. I delight in seeing young lovers court each other. There is caring, timing, joy and happiness. How they look into each other's eyes while peering into the depths of the soul. If there is no presence of light, they lovingly place some there. They radiate by every touch of the hand, every wink of the eye, glance from across the room and every exchange of thought. Their smile turns into laughter.

On the other hand, I have seen couples who have been married for a few years, dining at a restaurant: there is no conversation, no connection, as if there is no longer a feeling of love for each other. Where did it go? Who put the fire out? Could it be the guilt of past failures and the unwillingness to forgive? "I am amazed by how many individuals mess up every new day with yesterday. They insist on bringing into today the failures of yesterday, and in so doing they pollute a potentially wonderful day,"2 according to Gary Chapman.

Physical touch, words of affirmation, quality time, receiving gifts, and acts of service penned by Chapman as the five love languages, are all very effective ways of keeping the fires of love burning in the relationship with your spouse.

FORGET-ME-NOTS

- I delight in seeing young lovers court each other.
- Youthfulness in a relationship helps to keep the fires of love burning brightly.
- I have seen so many married couples who loose their zest, vim and vitality in their relationship right after the honey-moon.

"To create a relationship that takes you all the way to heaven, you have to accept your body completely. You have to love your body and allow your body to be free to just be, to be free to give, free to receive, without being shy, because 'shy' is nothing but fear"[1]

- Don Miguel Ruiz

10

The Romance Factor

Women want to be loved and cherished with a king to rule over them. Men want to be ad-mired and respected with a queen to support and motivate them. For her he will do any-thing. For him her senses will be aroused. I've chosen to dedicate this entire chapter to the relationship which exists in a marriage between a man and woman. Their God given bodies indicates that they were made for the other. Therefore, they should be sure to enjoy each other.

Romance in a marriage is like gasoline in a gas tank of an automobile and it's imperative to keep that love thank full. Most spouses destroy the romance in their affair by turning the relationship to quickly into a delegating of chores. They forget to laugh and have fun. Eat, pray, and play together. This will set the tone early for doing things together. Additionally, it will not only creates a romantic environment but develops a mindset for going through the storms of life together, when those storms arrive. In her bestseller The Total Woman Marabel Morgan writes an assignment for women entitled:

MAN ALIVE

1. Accept your husband just as he is. Write out two lists - one of his faults and one of his virtues. Take a long, hard look at his faults and then throw the list away; don't ever dwell on them again. Only think about his virtues. Carry that list with you and refer to it when you are mad, sad or glad.
2. Admire your husband every day. Refer to his virtue list if you need a place to start. Say something nice about his body today. Put his tattered ego back together with compliments.
3. Adapt to his way of life. Accept his friends, food, and lifestyle as your own. Ask him to write the six most important changes he'd like to see take place at your house. Read the list in private, react in private, and then

set out to accomplish these changes with a smile. Be a "Yes, let's!" woman some time of every day.

4. Appreciate all he does for you. Sincerely tell him "Thank you" with your attitudes, actions, and words. Give him your undivided attention, and try not to make any phone calls after he comes home, especially after 8:00 P.M.[2]

An associate of mine used to say that when a man comes home from work his wife ought to be dressed in her favorite nightwear, just finished reading a copy of The Total Woman. My associate's financial success will startle you, and has a wife whose submissiveness is unparalleled.

It would astonish you as to the number of women who would look their best when they go to their jobs and look the complete opposite when their husband comes home. Most women tend to let themselves go after they get the ring, they come to bed with rollers in their hair and holes under the armpit of their night attire. They care less about looking their best for the one they love. Men like to inspect what they expect and are therefore turned off instead of turned on fully by what they see. They still cherish being in bed with the beautiful angel, even more enhanced than when they first met. Eventually, and disappointingly they find themselves looking at another beauty instead of theirs.

On the other hand, most men do not take the time to set their wife's heart on fire by continually telling her how beautiful she is and how great she does the things that she do. "So far as loving is concerned, it is a man that makes a woman what she is by the way he treats her. He can bring out the bloom on her and help her reveal real charm."3 And "It is not only important that a man feel love for his wife, he must express it. This love can be expressed in a variety of ways, but since it is to be a daily practice, one can rely on words and tender affection. A man need not be adept with words as the poets to express the feelings in his heart."4 writes Dr. Aubrey Andelin.

I believe that if you like it you should tell her so. Maybe it is the sound of her voice, the sweep of her shoulders, the color of her eyes, her hair, and her cute smile and... She will love you more for doing so and it's sure better hearing it from you than from someone who does not have that intimate connection with her. You would be glad you did; you can be taken to a whole other level sexually.

The love letter philosophy

Many women love to see it in writing. To them, it is like a commitment of your love - now and forever. As a writer I tend to be more adept at writing than speaking, so here's one from my heart to hers.

My LOVE, I love you for who you are. I can't stop looking at you; you're more than a pleasure to behold. When you smile your lips not only move with the rhythm of your thoughts but your whole being gets into it.

When I look into your eyes I see a twinkle, and when you look back at me, in them I see the true color of love.

Today I reflected on how long and hard I'd searched, never knowing that I'd find someone like you. Now after so many years, you still possess my thoughts.

Thinking about you is automatic; the car you drive, its make and model, shows up every-where I go. Your passionate love and desire engulfs me.

I'm so proud to be loved by you. When you walk it's not a stroll but a stride filled with purpose and direction.

The sound of your voice…every syllable captivates me. I love the sweep of your shoulders, along with your gracious figure. Through the years you're still as beautiful as can be. You're more than a woman to me.

Now for the slight edge: Some might question "A love letter? It takes time to cohesively put all of those thoughts together to her. It may seem long but if you really love her it does not. First ask yourself "How much do I value this relationship?" and "Is this relationship price-less?

Women will spread love on when a man does something extra, or out of the norm to prove his love to her. They always seem to place more value in a flower, picked off the side of the road than a dozen red roses purchased from the nearby florist. Prove love - do these things for her and this next topic takes on a whole new meaning.

The three letter word in love

Sex still remains the most beautiful experience between a husband and wife. Sometimes wives complain that they do not get enough and husbands vice versa. Some wives make the sad mistake of depriving their husband sexually, with excuses such as having a headache. A devoted wife will take some painkillers and make her husband happy. When a man is undergoing a lot of stress he may have a small sexual appetite. If the woman is the cause of that stress, it could ruin their sexual experiences together.

Pastor Holly Wagner taught in her relationships seminar a few years ago about three different episodes of sex:

(1) The Snack,
(2) The Dinner and
(3) The Banquet.5

Marabel Morgan writes, "Tonight, as you make love, remember that your brain is your control center. Keep it tuned to the subject at hand. Think about his body, not Sunday's dinner menu. One of the secrets of life is to concentrate on the moment. Enjoy the present, not yesterday, or tomorrow, but right now! It's a secret to super sex, too."6 And Dr. David Reuben agrees: "The woman who would never think of serving her husband the same frozen television dinner every evening sometimes serves him the same frozen sexual response every night. Sex, like supper, loses much of its flavor when it becomes predictable. That, of course is the lure of the other woman; she offers the illusion that sex with her will be different. But if a wife is on the same emotional wave as her husband it will be hard for anyone else to provide greater satisfaction."7

FORGET-ME-NOTS

- A man's greatest desire is to make his wife happy and most men will if women will only let them.

- The better you get at having sex in the zone the better sex gets "like old wine with time."

- Sex still remains the most beautiful experience between a husband and wife.

- Women will spread love on when a man does something extra, or out of the norm to prove his love to her.

- I believe that if you like it you should tell her so.

- It would astonish you as to the number of women who'd look their best when they go to their jobs and look the complete opposite when their husband comes home.

*Give,
and it shall be given unto you;
good measure, pressed down,
and shaken together, and
running over, shall men give
into your bosom. For with the
same measure that ye mete
withal it shall be measured to
you again.*

Luke 6:38 KJV

11

The Philosophy of the Serve

It is a given that you can't give what you don't have and what you give you get: That's the philosophy of service. It is not what you do in a relationship. It is who you are and continues to be that matters.. According to Don Miguel Ruiz, M.D. in his book The Mastery of Love "The relationship you have with yourself is reflected in your relationship with others."1 In serving, one needs to focus on giving the maximum and not the minimum. The size of your love determines the size of your serve, which determines the size of your return.

The song "She believes in me" by Kenny Rogers encompasses the essence of this final chapter. Believing in YOURSELF has the power necessary to taxi down the runway but when someone else believes in you, the run-way can no longer hold you. In the movie "Rocky II" the character Rocky Balboa had lost not only the fight but also his self esteem. Even so, as soon as his wife expressed her belief in him, he became transformed and turned the fight's rematch into a win.

There's no "I" in team

It is fulfilling to watch a couple working together as a team, especially when they are doing it in sync. What they do is magnetic it draws you in.

Philip and Holly Wagner started the Oasis Christian Center in Los Angeles over 20 years ago. They were newlyweds and like most new couples, they struggled in their relationship with each other for several years. However, it is a joy to watch them work together, leading this 2,000 member church in the heart of the entertainment world - Hollywood.

I first met the duet over six years ago and became attracted to them instantly. There was a relational chemistry between them. Holly is like a cheerleader, while Philip is somewhat reserved. Yet their tremendous work-ethic in heading up a church which resembles the United Nations is amazing. Philip reiterates: "I love this church, walking through these doors energizes me."

After 23 years of marriage they still work on their relationship, and travel the world teaching others to do the same. Their love and respect for each other is like a transparent lacquer finish.

I remembered Holly telling a story about her teenage son when he was much younger. She states that one night after a busy day she was helping him with his homework and he was sassing her big time. Philip in another room overheard the exchange and emerged on the scene, to his son he echoed "Don't you ever talk to my wife like that again." His youngster got the message; that is teamwork in parenting. I have noticed their teamwork mindset and philosophy whether its raising funds for projects like: building water wells in Uganda or delivering the message on Sundays. Zinging each other from the seat is habitual.

A female group called "Godchicks" was start-ed by Holly a few years ago. These women meet several times a year and once annually for what's considered as their "Godchicks Conference" with Philip playing a very important role, not only as a speaker, but a promoter of the female gender.

Doing chores together erases the sneaky "I" in team and when mixed with prayer delivers creates a winning team - one to be reckoned with. "A family that prays together stays together" - Unknown.

Some men miss out on the blessings derived from staying alert to a woman's needs. Most women come prepared. Therefore, it's up to the man to study her area of expertise and weave them into their lives together. Which man can resist a growing woman, she's bound to get better all the time, if his phrases make her feel better about herself. The better the players play, the greater the team becomes.

A smart husband keeps his eyes open to those things which are particularly appealing and does not hesitate to let her know. Building up her strong points and not her faults puts her at ease and her respect for you and her work-ethic climbs to another level.

So, take charge, in love and when the times get tough and words are uttered like water from a dam, be both prepared to weather the storm. According to Shedd, on goals for communication, "We will remember that mystery is a blessing. Because it takes a lifetime to close all the gaps in the most perfect relationship we will be gentle. We will love to the fullest what is given today and expectantly wait for tomorrow"[2] Charlie W. Shedd.

Man's ability

A man's foremost and fundamental response to being honored is to serve. He has a tremendous capacity to be moved to greatness when his wife believes in him and tells him so. Many women do not realize this power within them. Therefore they miss out on the rewards that come when a man fulfils one of his greatest desires - achievement.

We all need to feel valued, to love and be loved everyday of our lives. When these needs are fulfilled we become our better selves. As a result, the world becomes a better place, our problems are minimized and we become more productive.

The love shared between two spouses is special and should last forever. It is your responsibility to treat it as such. If you want heat you have got to put wood in the stove and if you want continuous heat, you have got to continually put wood in the stove.

That is the power of the serve; what you give you get and it is worth repeating: the size of your love basically determines the power of your serve.

Small love = Small serve.
Big love = Big service.

Most of all! A man also has the ability to size up a situation very quickly - he's decisive by nature.

Though firm and courageous a good man also possesses tender qualities. This combination makes him very attractive to a woman. Genuine romantic love is usually stimulated by the woman - displaying all her feminine qualities.

A man can be an active participant if he fulfills his obligation by helping her to sparkle and shine as she once did. Women do not only need to hear daily "I love you." Some added expressions will add the feeling of love "You're beautiful, I love your hair, I love the scent of your perfume, your makeup is exquisitely done and on and on. "So far as loving is concerned, it is a man that makes a woman what she is by the way he treats her. He can bring out the bloom on her and help her reveal real charm. This is the miracle that cultivates your own feeling of love and tenderness for a woman"3 according to Dr. Aubrey Andelin. And Cecil G. Osborne states in For Men Only: "Treat your wife with strength and gentleness. No matter how self-reliant a woman may be; regardless of her intelligence, capability, and drive; even if she seems dominant there's something within her which wants to "lean" on a man. She would like to be swept off her feet, and then taken care of with gentleness and strength. This combination of strength and tenderness is not easily achieved if one does not possess it innately, but you can work on it. You may make mistakes, but with patience and determination you can satisfy your wife's inner need for emotional security with a quiet strength that is gentle and tender".4

Men are known to be logical while, women are emotional. In a sense they are like the tide and you just cannot predict if it is going to be high or low. Complicated as this may be, a man needs to learn how to be patient and considerate. In regard to her moods: "Ride them out with patience and kindly indulgence. Don't take it personally or tell her to 'snap out of it.'"5 Cecil G. Osborne.

Women seek reassurance. Telling her that you love her daily means a whole lot to her.

No matter how small the affection whether by words or touch, she thrives on it. The more wood you put in the stove the more heat will come your way. Also when you leave her presence you want to pour on your affection so that it will be nice and cozy when you return.

Tis the human touch in this world that counts
The touch of your hand and mine,
Which means far more than the fainting heart,
Than shelter and bread and wine ;
For shelter is gone when the night is o'er,
And bread lasts only a day,
But the touch of the hand
And the sound of the voice
Sing on in the soul away.6 -Spencer M. Tree

Man, the provider, protector, the builder of society, the guide, and the ball is in your hands. True growth comes only after you've moved beyond what you've already mastered.

THE CHAMPION

The average runner sprints
Until the breath in him is gone
But the champion has the iron will
That makes him "carry on.

For rest, the average runner begs
When limp his muscles grow
But the champion runs on leaden legs
His spirit makes him go.

The average man's complacent
When he does his best to score
But the champion does his best
And then he does a little more.

- Author unknown

If you're still holding on to your accomplishments of yesterday, release your grasp; it's time to move on. When you begin a new day, start it at a higher level of love. If you're in a valued relationship - that should be automatic. Your love of self and the one you love should grow daily. If not it is time to sharpen the "axe" through personal development - dozens of books have been written on relationships. Hone your craft; it's when you do the best that you can do that when genuine growth occurs.

It is also important to realize that you're not in a relationship to clean up what's wrong with your spouse. Instead, if you serve them well like a good quarterback, they will find a path to score the winning touchdown.

When God made the world he put man in charge of everything, including the woman. We live in a society where women complain that a "good man is hard to find." Men choose to stay single or form homogenous relationships; stating that they cannot find the right woman. Before your hunt for that mate begins, first hunt within yourself to ensure that what is inside you is something to be desired by the hunted.

No fisherman goes hunting with an empty hook and expects to catch fish; moreover the hook has to be baited with the right bait, based on the fish he desires to catch. No one hunts a deer with a sling shot, a gun is used instead. Therefore work steadfastly on yourself and become as powerful as the hunting weapon. "It is better to be prepared for an opportunity and not have one, than to have an opportunity and not be prepared."7 Whitney Young, Jr. and Benjamin Disraeli said: "One secret of success in life is for a man to be ready for his opportunity when it comes."8

After reading this book and applying its principles, your magnetism should cause others to befriend you and vice versa, and when this occurs, remember the philosophy of the serve, and serve them in the way that you'll like to be served. You will understand the importance of building a strong foundation in the early stages of your relationship. The famous axiom states: "It is not the height of your logic. It is the depth of your conviction." Be committed to building and the structure will get built.

To my sisters: You're valuable. Proverbs 31:10-31 (NIV) reads: "A wife of noble character who can find? She is worth far more than rubies. Her husband has full confidence in her and lacks nothing of value. She brings him good, not harm, all the days of her life. She selects wool and flax and works with eager hands. She is like the merchant ships, bringing her food from afar. She gets up while it is still dark; she provides food for her family and portions for her servant girls. She considers a field and buys it; out of her earnings she plants a vineyard. She sets about her work vigorously; her arms are strong for her tasks. She sees that her trading is profit-able, and her lamp does not go out at night. In her hand she holds the distaff and grasps the spindle with her fingers. She opens her arms to the poor and extends her hands to the needy. When it snows, she has no fear for her house-hold; for all of them are clothed in scarlet. She makes coverings for her bed; she is clothed in fine linen and purple. Her husband is respect-ed at the city gate, where he takes his seat among the elders of the land. She makes linen garments and sells them, and supplies the merchants with sashes. She is clothed with strength and dignity; she can laugh at the days to come. She speaks with wisdom, and faithful instruction is on her tongue. She watches over the affairs of her house-hold and does not eat the bread of idleness. Her children arise and call her blessed; her husband also, and he praises her: "Many women do noble things, but you surpass them all." Charm is deceptive, and beauty is fleeting; but a woman who fears the LORD is to be praised. Give her the reward she has earned, and let her works bring her praise at the city gate."

To my brothers, including those from another mother and father, this one is for you: "Nothing can turn a woman on quite like knowing that she turns you on"[9] Charlie W. Shedd.

FORGET-ME-NOTS

- No fisherman goes hunting with an empty hook and expects to catch fish; moreover the hook has to be baited with the right bait, based on the fish he desires to catch.

- When God made the world he put man in charge of everything, including the woman.

- It is also important to realize that you're not in a relationship to clean up what's wrong with your spouse.

- If you're still holding on to your accomplishments of yesterday, release your grasp; it's time move on.

- Women seek reassurance, telling her that you love her daily means a whole lot to her.

- Though firm and courageous a good man also possesses tender qualities.

- A man also has the ability to size up a situation very quickly – he's decisive by nature.

- A man has tremendous capacity to be moved to greatness when the woman in his life believes in him, and tells him so.

NOTES

Introduction

1. Alan Loy McGuiness, *The Friendship Factor,* (Minneapolis: Augsburg Publishing House, 1979), 51

Prelude to Chapter 1:

1. Napoleon Hill, *Think and Grow Rich,* (Chatsworth: Wilshire Book Company, 1999), 287

Chapter 1:

2. Ibid, 241-244
3. Gary Chapman, *The Five Love Languages,* (Chicago: Northfield Publishing, 2004), 19
4. Winner Quotes A-Z by Author, http://www.woopidoo.com/business_quotes/winning-quotes.htm
5. Love Styles, http://en.wikipedia.org/wiki/Love_styles
6. Abraham Lincoln, Abe Lincoln's Productivity Secret, http://www.persistenceunlimited.com/2006/01/abe-lincoln%E2%80%99s-productivity-secret/
7. Life of Dr. King, www.webstar.co.uk/~ubugaje/luther3.html

8. Martin Luther King, Jr. Biography, http://www.infoplease.com/spot/mlk biospot.html

9. Robert H. Schuller, *Self-Love* (New Jersey: Spire Books, 1969), 102-113

10. Alan Loy McGuiness, *Bringing Out The Best in People* (Minneapolis: Augsburg Publishing House, 1985), 44

Chapter 2:

1. Robert LeTournea, http://www.time.com/time/magazine/article/0,9171,942100,00.html

2. R. C. Allen, *The secret of Success* (Nevada: Best Books Inc. 1985), 113

3. Charlie W. Shedd, *Letters To Karen* (New York: Avon Books, 1968), 37

4. Ibid, 37

5. William Danforth, I Dare You (St Louis: American Youth Foundation, 1991), 10

6. Skip Ross with Carole C. Carlson, Say Yes to Your Potential (Rockford, MI: Circle "A" Productions, 1983), 92

7. Ibid, 92

8. Ibid, 92

9. Ibid, 91

10.Ibid, 60

Prelude to Chapter 3:

1. Ibid, 146

Chapter 3:

2. John Powell,S.J., *The Secret of Staying in Love,* (Allen: Tabor Publishing, 1974), 43

3. Les Brown, Live our Dreams, (New York: William Morrow & Company, Inc. 1992), 90

4. Ibid, 130

5. The Civil War Society's "Encyclopedia of the Civil War" http://www.civilwarhome.com/tubmanbio.htm

6. Skip Ross with Carole C. Carlson, 146-147

Prelude to Chapter 4:

1. Duane Hodgin, http://www.austinisd.org/academics/docs/CharacterEd_2005_03_respect_20050816.pdf

Chapter 4:

2. Dr. Emerson Eggerrichs, *Love & Respect,* (Nashville: Thomas Nelson, Inc. 2004), 271

3. Henry Wadsworth Longfellow, http://www.austinisd.org/academics/docs/CharacterEd_2005_03_respect_20050816.pdf

4. Dr. Emerson Eggerichs, *Love & Respect,* 7

5. Ibid, 183

6. Ibid, 35

7. George Washington, http://www.austinisd.org/academics/docs/CharacterEd_2005_03_respect_20050816.pdf

Prelude to Chapter 5:

1. Gary Chapman, *The Five Love Languages,* 39

Chapter 5:

2. John Maxwell & Les Parrott, 25 Ways To Win With People, 39

3. Elbert Hubbard, http://www.brainyquote.com/quotes/quotes/e/elberthubb122498.html

4. Aubrey Andelin, *Man of Steel and Velvet,* 218

5. Aubrey Andelin, *Man of Steel and Velvet,* 231

6. Les Giblin, *How To Have Power and Confidence In Dealing With People,*

(Englewood Cliffs: Prentice- Hall., Inc. 1956), 68

7. John Maxwell & Les Parrott, 25 Ways To Win With People, 174

8. Ibid, 174-175

9. Sydney J. Harris, http://www.barbaraglanz.com/newsletter/2007/03.html

10. Les Giblin, *How To Have Power and Confidence In Dealing With People,* 60

11. Ibid, 63

12. Ibid, 60

13. John Maxwell & Les Parrott, 25 Ways To Win With People, 122

14. Les Giblin, *How To Have Power and Confidence In Dealing With People,* XX

15. Ibid, 27

Prelude to Chapter: 6

1. Gary Chapman, *The Five Love Languages,* 20

Chapter 6:

2. Ralph Waldo Emerson, http://www.quotedb.com/quotes/1778

3. John Maxwell & Les Parrott, 25 Ways To Win With People, 104

Prelude to Chapter 7:

1. George T. Hewitt, http://www.quoteworld.org/quotes/6544

Chapter 7:

2. Gary Chapman, The Five Love Languages, 31

Prelude to Chapter: 8

1. Aubrey Andelin, Man of Steel and Velvet, 240

Chapter 8:

2. Aubrey Andelin, Man of Steel and Velvet, 341

Prelude to Chapter: 9

1. Aubrey Andelin, Man of Steel and Velvet, 235

Chapter: 9:

2. Gary Chapman, The Five Love Languages, 47

Prelude to Chapter 10:

1. Don Miguel Ruiz, The Mastery of Love, Amber - Allen Publishing, San Rafael, California. 1999, pg. 148

Chapter 10:

2. Marabel Morgan, Pocket Books, New York, NY. The Total Woman, 1973, 106 & 107

3. Aubrey Andelin, Man o f Steel and Velvet, 195

4. Aubrey Andelin, Man of Steel and Velvet, 195

5. Holly Wagner, Lord of the Rings relationship series, Oasis Christian Center, 2004.

6. Marabel Morgan, The Total Woman, 158

7. Marabel Morgan, The Total Woman, 156

8. Marabel Morgan, The Total Woman, 159 & 160

Chapter 11:

1. Don Miguel Ruiz, The Mastery Of Love, 148

2. Shedd, Letters To Philip, 28

3. Aubrey Andelin, Man of Steel and Velvet, 195

4. Cecil Osborne, Edited by J Allan Petersen, For Men Only, Living Books, Tyndale House Publishers, Wheaton, Illinois. 1973, 76

5. For Men Only, Cecil Osborne, 80

6. Man of Steel and Velvet, Aubrey Andelin, 217

7. Whitney Young Jr. http://www.wow4u.com/opportunity/index.html

8. Benjamin Disraeli. http://www.brainyquote.com/quotes/quotes/b/benjamindi130016.html

9. Letters To Philip, Shedd, 47

ABOUT THE BOOK

SPREAD SOME LOVE (Relationships 101) was born out of his failed marriage which ended after 13 years in 2000. Since then John has not only read dozens of books on relationships but has associated with several experts on this subject, including Pastor's Philip and Holly Wagner, whose marriage is now entering half a century. As an entrepreneur and sought after coach, Mr. Andrews believes that marriages should last forever and states: "If a person isn't willing to work on him or herself they should stay out of the falling in love business; the world is full of too many abandoned relation-ships and broken hearts."

Single Letter Characters

Mr. X..The Author

The following names were used to protect the identity of those individuals.

Ms. A
Mr. Y.
Mr. Z.

Double Letter Characters

W.B.
T.W.

Available Services

Consulting and training sessions are available for groups as well as individuals.

For more information contact us via Email: john@btweyl.info Or visit us at www. AndrewsLeadershipInternational.com

---

NEED A SPEAKER FOR YOUR EVENT?

Interested in having author John A. Andrews or another speaker from Andrews Leadership International to speak at your event about:

Leadership For EVER

- EMPOWERMENT
- VISION
- ENTERTAINMENT
- RELATIONSHIPS

ABOUT THE AUTHOR

Prolific, National Bestselling Author John A. Andrews, screenwriter, producer, and author of several books, founded Teen Success in 2009. Its mission statement: ***To invigorate and stimulate teens to maximize their full potential, to be successful and become contributing citizens in the world***. As an author of books on relationships, personal development, and vivid engaging stories, John is sought after as a motivational speaker to address success principles to young adults. John makes an impact in the lives of others because of his passion and commitment to make a difference in the world. Being a father of three sons propels John even more in his desire to see teens succeed. Andrews, a divorced dad of three sons ages 14, 12 and 10, was born in the Islands of St. Vincent and the Grenadines. He grew up in a home of five sisters and three brothers. He recounts: "My parents were all about values: work hard, love God and never give up on dreams."

Self educated, John developed an interest for music. Although lacking the formal education he later put his knowledge and passion to good use, moonlighting as a disc jockey in New York. This paved the way for further exploration in the entertainment world. In 1994 John caught the acting bug. Leaving the Big Apple for Hollywood over a decade ago not only put several national TV commercials under his belt but helped him to find his niche.

His passion for writing started in 2002, when he was denied the rights to a 1970's classic film, which he so badly wanted to remake. In 2007, while etching two of his original screenplays, he published his first book "The 5 Steps to Changing Your Life" Currently he's publishing his fifteenth volume, while working on empowering teens worldwide.

In 2008 he not only published his second book but also wrote seven additional books that year, and produced the docu-drama based on his second book, *Spread Some Love (Relationships 101).*

See Imdb: http://www.imdb.com/title/tt0854677/.

"Some people create, while others compete. Creating is where the rubber meets the road. A dream worth having is one worth fighting for because freedom is not free; it carries a massive price tag."

* * *

New Release

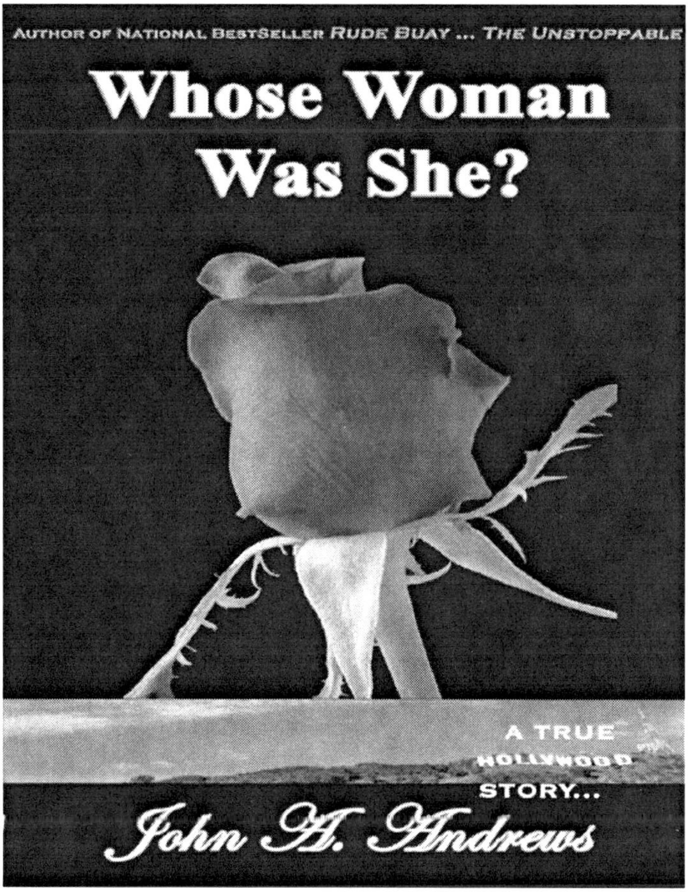

A BIOGRAPHICAL THRILLER

Before that thought perished, my house phone rang. It dawned on me, whoever was trying to reach her, was also trying to reach me as well. I released my arms from around Eve, and reluctantly reached for the phone.
"Like a Devil In Disguise" she belonged to someone else, not to another man. Whose woman was she?

CHICO RUDO ... EL IMPARABLE

Autor John A. Andrews, hijo de la tierra Caribeña, penetra en el vientre del mundo de la droga. En un ambiente saturado con la corrupción, el engaño, duplicidad, engaño y las desigualdades de todo tipo, Andrews concibe una Cruz Atlántico, codicia, impulsado por el fracaso, incrustados en la epidemia de drogas. ¿Puede Jamaicano nacido, DEA "Chico Rudo", guardar su país de la tiranía del Cartel de drogas de dragón?

COMING SOON

CROSS ATLANTIC FIASCO

National Bestselling Author

of

RUDE BUAY ... THE UNSTOPPABLE

粗魯的男孩 … …不可阻擋

¿CUYA MUJER FUE ELLA?

LOS CINCO "PS" PARA ADOLESCENTES

DARE TO MAKE A DIFFERENCE
SUCCESS 101
THE TEACHER'S GUIDE

5 PASOS PARA CAMBIAR SU VIDA

QUOTES UNLIMITED II

WHO SHOT THE SHERRIFF?

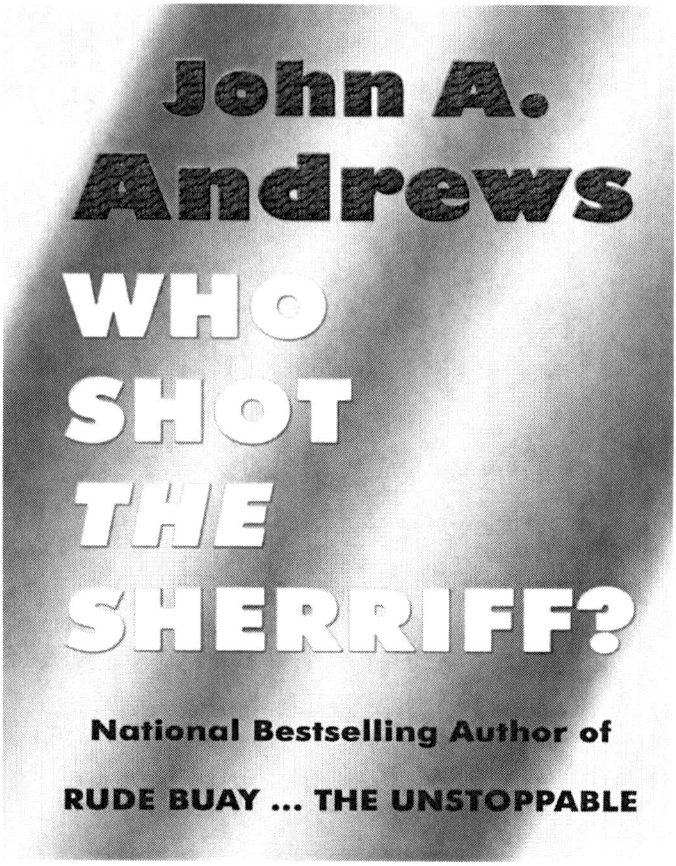

THE CLOSING DOORS

MAXIMIZE YOUR POTENTIAL SIGNIFICANCE 101

There are things you and I will accomplish in our lifetime that will not only astonish our relatives, friends, neighbors, co-workers but our enemies alike. It has been discovered that 90% of an iceberg rests beneath the surface. It may surprise you that each of us has at least 90% of our potential lying untapped. As human beings, we are known to only use that other 10% of our potential. Like going from good to great, the high achievers in life attain their highest heights by going from success to significance. At this level, their destiny not only embodies greatness but true significance; they add value to others. The well known axiom states: Success is adding value to self, significance is adding value to others. The successful achieves significance by tapping deeper and deeper into their unused capacity.

In my interaction with people of significance, I've discovered that they are not only specialists in their field. At one point in their lives they said yes to their potential. As visionaries, they continue to empower others to maximize their God given potential. They realize that they don't have a thousand years to live, so they do all they can with their time, money and skills. They abhor going to their graves with their music leashed.

You too can join the significant by simply saying yes to your God given potential.

"QUOTES" Unlimited.

Quotes from my treasury and 101 Quotes Which Inspired Me.

"If we think with a mindset of giving, we entertain abun-dance, and if we think with an attitude of withholding, we invite lack. As the source gives to the stream so ought the stream to impart to the ocean."

_ John A. Andrew

THE 5 STEPS TO CHANGING YOUR LIFE

"THE 5 STEPS TO CHANGING YOUR LIFE" In this book , John A. Andrews takes you on a journey from the inside out, extracting insights from his own life and great inspirational literature, most of them written several decades before he was born - delivering nugget after nugget of wisdom - essential for changing your life as well as impacting your world. So many embark upon the task of revolutionizing their home, their church and their world but never start with the "self." Everything you see on the outside first came from within. Real change is an "inside job." Learn the five fundamental steps necessary and pass it on to others.

TOTAL COMMITMENT - THE MINDSET OF CHAMPIONS

Action is a doing word! Once you acquire this habit, others have no choice but to step aside for you. You are now a crusader, and the world always seems to make way for the person who knows where he or she is going.

HOW I WROTE 8 BOOKS IN ONE YEAR

Writing my first book did not only cause me tap into my unused potential, but brought me off the sidelines and into the game. I decided that no one was going to outwork me. Since I had never taken a typing class, I was not adept at using the computer's keyboard. My word per minute was about a few words a minute. Someone once said: *When the dream is big*

enough the facts don't count. In the summer of 2008, I wrote, published, and released *Spread Some Love (Relationships 101).*

It's my belief that if my thoughts can produce it, it can be written.

SPREAD SOME LOVE - RELATIONSHIPS 101

DOCU-DRAMA

This 60 minute slice of life Docu-drama comes filled with beats cemented in relational mystique. This DVD features elite relationship interviews, dramatic scenes, unique historical footage, sizzling music and much more.

SPREAD SOME LOVE - RELATIONSHIPS 101

WORKBOOK

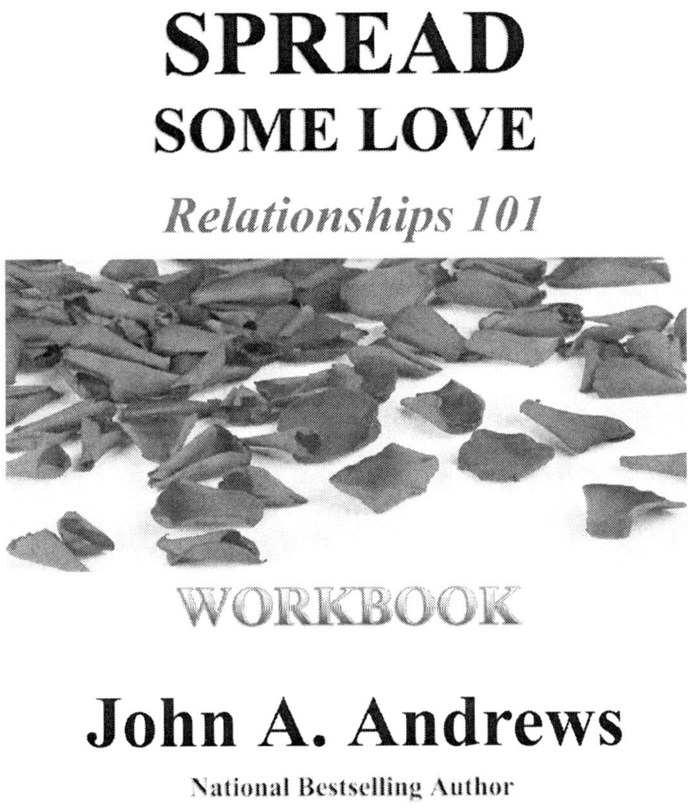

Three weeks after the release of the foundation to this workbook "Spread Some Love (Relationships 101)," I was doing a book signing event at a restaurant in Southern California. A woman came up to me and asked if she can scan through my new volume. I enthusiastically gave her the go ahead. Before wrapping the event some two hours later, I noticed that she was not only still holding the book in her hands but was joined by four other women - all in their late 20's to early 30's. I stepped into their space and after introducing myself, joined their huddle. I asked where everyone was in their relationships with a significant other. I learned that two of them were married, two were still single and one was going through a divorce – they weren't very passionate about their relational status.

The woman going through her divorce asked me what motivated me to write such a book. I responded enthusiastically: "Doctors go to school for a reason, so do lawyers, pastors keep studying in order to remain on the pulpit but we fail to work on our relationships on a daily basis. Many of us fall in love and expect that osmosis will pull every-thing together. It doesn't - It can't." She sobbingly echoed: "where were you a year ago." That hit home. A year too late I pondered - her marriage would have been saved. **Writing this workbook was inescapable!**

SPREAD SOME LOVE - RELATIONSHIPS 101

THE 52 WEEK JOURNAL

This JOURNAL comes sugared with eclectic quotes, poems, forget-me-nots and extra space to inscribe your everyday thoughts or ideas.

DARE TO MAKE A DIFFERENCE (SUCCESS 101)

For what do I want to be remembered? This is a fundamental question asked by just about every successful individual, because like the caterpillar going through the cocoon to become a beautiful butterfly, equally, all truly successful people go through walls which stood in their way towards their destiny. They will also tell you that their success principles were rooted deep inside of them and were the defining agents which helped create the success that you see all around them. If you nurture those roots which run deep within you, your chance of succeeding is inevitable.

THE 52 WEEKS GOAL SETTING QUEST

QUOTES FROM MY TREASURY

THE SUCCESS TRIANGLE

Many people get knocked down and remain in that fetal position, fearing to take another blow from the storms of life.

Conversely, the high achievers in life get back up and fight the good fight in pursuit of the prize. In 2000, I hit rock bottom after my divorce. Subsequently, many forces tried to keep me down. I knew possessed value and if I persisted and persevered, value would surface, blessing the lives of many, including those who I may never meet.

The Success Triangle™ features 3 of my books. By writing these pages, my life has turned from one of divorce and loneliness to being embraced by the world. As a token of gratitude, I therefore pass them on to you, hoping that you will discover your own magic and embark upon your life's mission, daring to make a difference.

RUDE BUAY ... THE UNSTOPPABLE

Author John A. Andrews, son of the Caribbean soil, penetrates inside the belly of the drug world. In an environment saturated with corruption, deception, duplicity, deceit, and inequities of all kinds, Andrews conceives a cross Atlantic, greed driven fiasco, embedded within the drug epidemic. Can Jamaican born, DEA "Rude Buay," save his country from the tyranny of the Dragon Drug Cartel?

DARE TO MAKE A DIFFERENCE - SUCCESS 101 FOR TEENS

Dare to Make a Difference - Success 101 For Teens is rich and full of history. Saturated, with stories about high achievers, who have daringly blazed the trails of success. Their chronicles are arranged buffet style, with something for everyone. Some accounts are short, funny, witty, thrilling, long, dramatic, daring, and to the point. Most of all they lend support to anyone bent on success.

The FIVE "Ps" For Teens

The 5 Traits every teen should know and have

CONTACT INFORMATION

For more information about *JOHN A. ANDREWS*, to book speaking engagements, sign up for his mailings, purchase his books and to learn more about other BOOKS THAT WILL ENHANCE YOUR LIFE ™, visit his website at:

www. Theteensuccess.com
EMAIL
john@theteensuccess.com
or

Contact John at:

BOOKS THAT WILL ENHANCE YOUR LIFE™
www.booksthatwillenhanceyourlife.com

BOOKS THAT WILL ENHANCE YOUR LIFE

NOTES

NOTES

NOTES

NOTES

NOTES

NOTES

NOTES

NOTES

CPSIA information can be obtained at www.ICGtesting.com
Printed in the USA
LVOW040311081111

253994LV00003B/23/P

9 780983 845768